WHY I DON'T WRITE LIKE FRANZ KAFKA

Why I Don't Write
Like Franz Kafka

William S. Wilson

The Ecco Press   New York

Library of Congress Cataloging in Publication Data
Wilson, William S.   1932–
   Why I don't write like Franz Kafka.
   Contents: Love.—Marriage.—Men.—Women.—Motherhood.
—Fatherhood.—Desire.—America.—Métier.—History.—
Anthropology.—Interim.—Conveyance.
   I. Title.
PZ4.W7545Wh   [PS3573.I4764]   813.'5'4   77-71284
ISBN 0-912-94641-5 (hardbound)
      0-912-94642-3 (paperbound)

Grateful acknowledgment is made to the following publications in
which these stories first appeared: *Antaeus:* "America," "Anthropol-
ogy," "History," "Interim," "Love," "Marriage," "Men," "Métier:
Why I Don't Write Like Franz Kafka." *New Directions in Prose and
Poetry 33:* "Fatherhood," "Motherhood." *Paris Review:* "Conveyance."
Tri Quarterly: "Desire."

For my mother and my father

CONTENTS

WHY I DON'T WRITE LIKE FRANZ KAFKA

LOVE

"I have been haunted by a topological conjecture . . . Yet I can find neither proof nor counterexample. It seems the time has come to abjure vanity, and pose the question for someone else to answer. I will try to pose it in mathematically precise terms in three parts. . . ."

—A. T. WINIFREE,
"Patterns of Phase Compromise in Biological Cycles,"
Journal of Mathematical Biology 1, #1 (1974).

I. IF LOVE IS CONSISTENT, IT IS INCOMPLETE.

I love you.

All right, but don't say it so often.

Why not?

Because this is an illusion.

What is?

Love. You and me.

Us?

No, there's no us. Just you and me.

Why does it make you so angry?

Because it isn't real. There is no *us*, there's you and there's me. There is something between us, I admit that I feel it, but it isn't love. It can't be, because there's no such thing. Love is an illusion.

If you mean that you don't love me, say so. Remember, we were going to say what we feel.

I can't feel what doesn't exist.

I love you.

Stop saying that. You don't know what you're talking about.

I think I do. I believe that I love you, and you can't deny

[1]

that you've been investigating the possibility that you love me, and the effect of your investigations of feelings, at least for me, has been to bring the feelings into existence. I have found out what I feel.

Listen, we're two different people.

Of course. I love you, not me. I'm not very lovable.

Of course you're lovable.

You've made me feel that at times, but now you say that love is an illusion.

Maybe I mean that we expect too much from it. You overestimate its power. You enlarge love until I see the flaws in it. Don't overdo it. When you believe in love so much I have to warn you, and maybe warn myself, it's an illusion.

I accept it as I find it.

But we didn't just find it. Whatever we have, we have constructed by probing. I'm questioning whether we've constructed anything objective.

It feels objective to me. I am constrained to think of you in a certain way, and I have feelings for you, new feelings, which are like theorems that come into existence as they are proved. We don't have our feelings until we examine them and find out what they are.

You can't prove them. They don't exist.

I don't see how you can doubt them, and I don't see how you can doubt your feelings without thinking that they must exist in order for you to doubt them. I can't blame you for doubting my statements about love, but I don't think you have any grounds for doubting my love, and I don't know why you want to. If you'll listen, I'll prove to you that what you say about what I say about love is true.

[2]

LOVE

Then you're agreeing with me.

Not at all. I might agree with you on statements about love, and not agree with you about love.

I'm not sure now that I want to win this argument.

You can decide when you see what the argument was. Your purpose in starting an argument with me will find itself serving purposes you can't know until you reach them. The question whether you have lost or won may not be answered by this argument.

I'm waiting for you to prove that you love me, and that what I say about love is true.

We'll start with statements about love. Suppose we take a statement, and to identify it we give it a name. The statement *Love is not provable* we will name after itself, and put the name in quotation marks, so *"Love is not provable"* is the name of the statement *Love is not provable*. We could give the name of the statement a name, but we won't need to tonight.

I am fond of you, you know.

That will probably help the argument. Let's take another statement, *Love has no meaning*, and name that statement *"Love has no meaning."* Then we can take the statement *Love has no meaning*, and substitute a variable X for *love*. Then we have not a statement but a statement-form: *X has no meaning*.

I follow. X is the variable, and *X has no meaning* is the statement-form and not the statement because it contains a variable.

Right. And we can change the statement-form back into a statement by making a substitution for the variable X, and one of the substitutions can be the name of the statement-form substituted for the variable in the statement-form. So if the name of *X has no meaning* is *"X has no meaning"* we can substitute the name for the variable, and then we get *"X has no meaning" has no meaning.*

I understand. And if I said that love is not provable, you could say *"Love is not provable" is not provable.*

I could also say *"Love is not provable" is provable.* But we'd better go back to our incomplete statement and admit that it is indemonstrable; we can't prove the statement we get when we substitute the name of the statement-form for the variable in the statement-form *X is not provable.*

You must love me to go to this trouble.

You mean that you're getting tired. But we're almost finished. We just said of a statement that it can't be proved.

It wasn't a statement, it was a statement-form, because it had a variable X. You see, I am paying attention.

Good. Now we need to find out what the statement is that we have been talking about, so we replace the variable with the name of the statement-form. The statement we get by substituting in the statement-form *X is not provable* the name of the statement-form is the sentence *"X is not provable" is not provable.* If that statement is true, we can prove it only if it is false, and if it's false, it's unprovable.

Are you arguing fairly?

Yes. Remember that we agreed that we cannot prove the statement that we get when we substitute for the variable in the statement-form X the name of the statement-form. Now if we take that statement, and name it after itself, and substitute the name for the variable, we have to say, *We can't prove the statement which we get by substituting for the variable in the statement form "We can't prove the statement which we get by substituting for the variable in the statement-form X the name of the statement-form" the name of the statement-form.*

So the statement says that it can't be proved?

Yes, it's a little like when I tell you that I believe your lies, or when you say that everything you say is wrong. I can say that your statement, *Love has no meaning*, has no meaning, but I can't prove it without talking nonsense, and I can say that your statement *Love is an illusion* is an illusion, but I can't prove it without seeing the illusoriness of my statements.

Then everything I say about the meaninglessness of love is not meaningless. You think that *Love has no meaning* has no meaning, and *Love is an illusion* is an illusion, and *Love is not provable* is not provable, unless it is true, but if it's true, it is not provable. And if it's false it's not provable because we can't prove a false statement to be true. So you can't prove that I'm wrong.

True. But you can't prove that you're right. We cannot prove the statement that we cannot prove statements about love.

So we can't prove or disprove them?

Not in this language.

Is there any other?

Certainly. We could invent one. I've been proving that statements about love are demonstrable and indemonstrable; I haven't proved anything about love.

Then what are you saying?

[5]

I think you know. What do you think I'm saying?

That's not a fair question. Not yet. I can't tell whether I'm winning or losing this argument, or whether I want to win or lose. How do I decide that?

You can't decide that in the language we've been using. The question whether or not love has meaning can't be decided in the language we've been using because the meaning of that language is outside the language itself.

Where is it?

I think you know. You've been looking for the proof of the meaning of our statements about love in other statements. I say *I love you* so often that the sentence becomes depleted and you begin to doubt it. I've shown you that you're entitled to doubt the statement because I can't prove it with other statements, but you are entitled to doubt only the language I use for love, not the feeling. We have to decide about the feeling in another language that is another form of proof.

I think I'd like to speak it with you now.

II. OR

I love you without illusion now.

You're proud of yourself for that.

Meaning?

Meaning you love the way you love me, but you have subtracted a few illusions from your perception of me and added a few to your perception of yourself. I have to be what you think you see in me, and I'm not that, and you refuse to see it. You flatter yourself if you think you see me as I am,

without flattery. I'm as tired of being overestimated by you as I am of being underestimated by other people.

What do you want me and the other people to do?

I want you to try seeing me as you see me, and as I see myself, and as I am. Stop seeing how beautifully you see me. What you mean when you say that you love me without illusion is that you see faults in me that you don't like but that you love me anyway. Loving your loving is not the same as loving me, and it leaves me as lonely as before.

You're being complicated about what could be as simple as the fact that you don't love me.

There, you are doing it again, preferring what you think I feel to what I feel. If you want to know whether or not I love you, ask me. If you have to ask. But please don't prefer what you think I think or feel to what I think or feel. And anyway you are wrong, I do love you, and that's the trouble. We both know there's something wrong. I love you, I love you, you love me, you love me. Don't you feel the tautology? I love you because you are lovable and because you love me, and I love myself because I am loved, and everything is lovely. There's no friction.

You're not telling me anything except that you're bored, and that I make you feel boring. You can't stand not being entertaining and interesting. Or feeling that you aren't.

That's not a very lovable remark. I'm not bored. Maybe I'm making you feel boring, have you thought of that? And instead of admitting it, and accusing me, you accuse me of accusing you. I don't want to be blamed for your feelings. I'm trying to rub some color over our feelings to bring up

the outlines of ideas. That way we can think about our feelings together.

I don't think I want to see the feelings under these ideas.

Look, do you think I want to? I do love you, but we're so far into love that we've touched some limit or boundary, and maybe there's nothing beyond it. Or perhaps the space of love is curved and we've come back upon ourselves too soon. We've proved we love each other, and now what?

I think you're proving that you don't.

Don't oversimplify. We have a problem and I want to understand it. We have been happy and we could be happy again.

I don't want to think about it.

We are thinking about it, whether we know it or not. I want to know it. We agreed long ago to find the axioms of our love. We assumed at the beginning that a fitting and formal language was worth looking for.

Love is not a fiction of logic.

And every axiom of our love would be a tautology, and with a set of rules of transformation we could derive theorems and formulas. If the axioms are consistent, then the love would be consistent.

It would be, if you would leave it alone.

It is consistent, I can prove that. If the axioms were inconsistent, then any formula at all could be derived from them, and they would all be tautologies. If there is a formula that is not a theorem, not derived from the axioms, then the axioms are consistent.

Would you repeat that?

No, I think you heard me. If we can find a formula that is

[8]

not derived from the axioms, that is not a tautological theorem, then the axioms are consistent because there is a formula
that is not derived from the axioms; and if the axioms
weren't consistent, any formula would be a theory and a
tautology, because any formula could be derived from inconsistent axioms.

Have you found what it is that you're looking for?

Yes, a formula that is not a tautology. I have one: "Either
p or q."

What of it?

That formula is not a tautology, so it isn't derived from
the axioms, and therefore they are consistent. Therefore the
axioms of our love are consistent.

But "p or q" contains variables. What are you substituting
for the variables? What does your formula have to do with
me?

Simply this. When we substitute ourselves for the variables,
then we have a formula that isn't derived from the axioms:
"Either you or me."

III. POSSIBILITY

I don't want any more logical fictions. I am foolish enough
to say that I want your love. I am not going to betray my
feelings. I am using all of my strength to reveal this weakness, because we agreed once to tell the truth and not to be
facetious or ironic. That sometimes left us with not much to
say. I love you, but I have nothing to do with whether or
not I am loved, and I'm not going to say or do anything to
make you love me. I am not going to humor you, or maneuver
or manipulate your feelings. You have to do as you please

without help from me, because I want your free choice of me. I am not going to give you any encouragement.

Suppose I could prove that you are lovable.

Would it make any difference?

It would make a difference to me.

It would make a difference to me too, but don't say anything because you think it's what I want to hear. I want you to do what you want to do, and I admit that I want that to be loving me. I have to feel that you are free to choose so that I can feel you choosing me. Nothing less will reach me.

You're adorable.

So I have been told. It hasn't made me happy.

You are also lovable and nonlovable.

I know that I am not lovable. It's the theory of myself that most experience has confirmed. The news is that I'm not trying to be lovable.

You are lovable, and I'll show you how.

I'm willing to listen.

First we have to think of a class which is a member of itself, like the class of thinkable things, and of a class which is not a member of itself, like the class of dogs, which is not a dog.

All right. I like the thought of the class of thinkable things.

Suppose we think of the class of all lovable things.

I can see it. What I need to know is whether or not I am in it.

Be patient. Is the class of all lovable things lovable?

Certainly. I wouldn't hate all lovable things, so I wouldn't hate the class of all lovable things. But I want to feel free to change my mind about it later.

[10]

LOVE

So the class of all lovable things is lovable and is a member of itself.

Yes, if that's what I've agreed to. I'm trying to picture me to myself inside it or outside it. And I'm trying to picture me to you as self-centered, I hope you haven't missed that.

So "lovable" is a member of the class "lovable"?

Why not? Is there any reason why it shouldn't be?

So "lovable" is "lovable."

When you put it that way, I don't think I like it.

So now we have the class of all lovable things, which is lovable, and is a member of itself, but you don't like that it is lovable, so the class of all lovable things, if it is lovable, is not lovable, so it is not a member of itself if it is a member of itself.

If you say so. Does this have anything to do with me?

You are for me in the class of lovable things.

Which makes me nonlovable, if I've kept up with current events. I've always felt that. Don't put your hand there.

The argument makes you nonlovable only if you are lovable.

I'm not trying to be lovable.

Exactly. You wouldn't be lovable if you weren't nonlovable.

But there's nothing exact about it. I think that love is in the class of unthinkable things, and I don't know how to think about it. One of us denied once that love exists. I don't remember who.

It might have been either of us.

It was you. And now you're trying to get around feelings with logic, instead of coming through the feelings to actions.

[11]

No, I'm telling you that I love you more than logic, because when I say that you are in the class of nonlovable things, I mean that I find inconsistency again. I feel the space that curves around us, and yet I feel a space between us also.

You're telling me that you love me, and I'm warning you that I love you too much and desire your love too much to make myself lovable to you. I will be unlovable if I want to. You have to decide without my help. It's going to take truth to satisfy my desire.

Yes, I know that. I love you for that.

Are you touching me because you want to or because you know that I want you to?

Both.

MARRIAGE

I wake, though not as after sleep. Each muscle of my body is articulated. An anatomy lesson. I can feel intersections of pain, and across my chest a concavity around which I breathe uneasily. I think to myself, it must be the valves. My mouth is open and dry, my eyes closed and sullen, my fingers muffled and blunt. I feel one hand with the other, and they rub like a shroud against a shroud, for both hands are bandaged. I raise a hand to my face, and again bandage rubs against gauze. I glide, my body spins into the outline of pain, and then its empty aura. I sleep, bandaged and enfolded.

I hear distant voices asking questions, voices asking tenderly, commanding gently, voices professionally asking and answering remotely. A man's voice, a woman's voice, a man's voice asking questions, a woman's voice answering, and then amplifying her answer. I feel unequal to myself and lapse into sleep.

Awake again, I am contracted to the present. Feelings stick to me. Pain adheres. I can tell from the skin on my face that the bandages are gone, but my eyes are closed and I can't pull the lids open or locate the muscles that would raise my eyelids. My hands are bandaged, my eyes will not open, my mouth is dry. I want to speak, but I cannot move my tongue beyond rha, arh, uh, runh. Someone's body pushes lightly against the side of the bed, a few drops of water touch my tongue, my mouth is absorbed in its own stale tastes.

It's my side. I have found the pain. It is in my side, and I isolate it and define it, and arrange the other pains around it. I tell myself that pain is information, that I am learning to map the spaces of my own body. Then my body's feelings cascade toward my side, and pain pours over its outlines and erases them.

Ruhn, I say, arhn, and someone drops water into my mouth, wet fingers touch my forehead with a cloth; dry cotton probes my ears. I cannot hear the voices clearly, and cannot lift my body to turn. Then hands lift my hands, unwrap the bandages, and I reach out to stretch my arms. My left hand touches another body.

A hand removes my hand from that flesh, a blanket and sheet are pulled up, and my hands are folded on my chest and patted. I can feel the edges of the blanket and sheet squeezed in my left hand, which makes a fist. I bite my lower lip. Pains unfurl from my left side.

The pain does not hurt me so much as what I know. The body beside me in the bed is the body of the only woman, and my body lying next to hers—my eyes sewn shut like a falcon's, my tongue tied down with surgical thread, my hands baffled by uncertainty—is keeping her alive. She is grafted onto me, and through the extension of my veins and intestines, joined to hers by a hinge of flesh, she shares my life. The pains in my legs subside, the pains in my muscles fade, and I stop picturing myself as a pounding, asymmetrical heart about to burst. I know what I am doing, and I can bend my elbows, breathe deeply, and rock my head slowly from side to side, splashing peripheral light into the central darkness.

Nothing needs explaining, I know what to do. As the pain recedes, as days or nights pass, as I am spoken to, I know what my task is. One day arms lift and turn me, awaking pain which clarifies the awkward shape of my body. I sit on the edge of the bed, my legs over the side; slippers are hung on my feet, and then I am pushed until my feet touch the floor and I stand up. We stand up. My hands are untied but motionless. A hand pushes on my back, I shuffle forward. The slippers scratch at the floor, and I learn from their sound to pick up my feet. I am glad no one in that room can see me as I see myself in lineaments of pain.

I am backed onto a chair, and then I, then we, then she and I are wheeled, sitting on a double chair, down a hallway, through abrupt echoes, across the passerelle between wings of the hospital, and into the solarium. I know the room, or I knew it once, as wicker furniture, dusty artificial anemones in a vase, and a cool tile floor. When I sat in that room before, I looked down into the street below, at the windows of the stationery store, the coffee shop, the florist. I used to go into shops where I was recognized to make small unnecessary purchases.

But now we are wheeling into the sunlight, and out of the sunlight, and one day we wheel ourselves, and then one later day we wheel across to the solarium, are helped out of the chair, are helped to learn to get out of the chair together and without help, and we learn to walk, to sit, to turn toward each other and away from each other without strain. One day we walk without the chair, we stroll across the corridor, and from that day I look forward to the hallway windows which provide serial gradations of sight.

Then one day, without warning, down in the elevator and out to the street, with noise crowding my movement, and camera flashbulb lights pinking in my eyes, and I know myself only as a desire to scream contained in a body which is screaming. I feel that my body is audible, my heartbeat visible, and the registrations of my pain tangible, but I am certain that no one notices. I try and fail to feel brave, and then by an effort I subtract myself from the scene, leaving a mere shape in the laminations of light on a metropolitan street at midday.

The other days repeat a few formations, a series of rehearsed movements, inversions and reversals. But one episode from the night will put the woman in a better perspective. I have been sleeping, and am awakened by a woman's hand on my chest, her breath against my neck, her lips to my skin, and an earnest pressure that is almost a pain in the hinge that extends from my side into hers. The fingers touch the hair on my forehead, trace my nose and lips, and draw along my chest. But I know well enough the operations necessary to my body if it is to support both our lives, and the hand that searches down my stomach and approaches across my thigh touches vacancy.

I have shown no sign of being awake or aware, and have felt almost nothing. She kisses my shoulder and eases her-

self back until she is lying flat again. I would not measure the
months or years since then, but my heart is swollen now,
my body seems to have ripened inside, and then overripened.
I am almost too heavy to be lifted out of bed, and surely cannot sustain two lives much longer. I know what this means
for me. I will miss sitting in the solarium, I suppose, but
except for the solarium, I can't say that I have cared where
I have been or when, or what I have eaten. I was bothered
once by wet feet, and my nails were allowed to grow too
long. I scratched the backs of my hands until they were infected. When the nails were trimmed the hands healed. The
irritation on my hands was interesting as long as it lasted.

Now I can feel in her like the pull of tides something con-
cave longing for convexity. I am strong enough to feel in
her body a need which my body is too weak to satisfy. One
day we will sit together on the chair again, I will focus far
behind my eyes, and then we, then she and I, will be wheeled
away and I will sleep into detachment.

MEN: THE MAN WHO
ENDS HIS STORY

I. HIS STORY SO FAR

A doctor in a hospital has presented to a board of doctors for diagnosis and prognosis an alien Caucasian male aged thirty-eight, brought to the hospital feigning a disability and living on the compensation for it. The patient was found to be in good general health, although he continued to complain of distress and pain which were diagnosed as functional since no physiological or structural cause was apparent.

He protested his detainment with the other patients, and said that all he asked was entrée into a living continuum, or, failing that, an introduction into the discontinuations and discontinuities of death. The doctors, unsure of his meaning, variously proposed operations that would induce giantism so that he would feel himself growing again, an operation that would transform him into a woman capable of bearing a child, an operation in which he would experience a few seconds of death and then be resuscitated. The patient complained that none of the doctors had introduced himself to him or asked him his name. He said that they would be answerable to others for the jealous guard they kept over death, and that they would have to answer to themselves for their attempts to protect patients from pain.

The patient, who claims to have a wife and two children, expressed dissatisfaction with the relationships. He spoke reasonably. He regretted some of his criticisms, but wanted to get one thing fitted into its proper and permanent place before he died; and should that not be possible, he would be satisfied if he could know how the story of his life ended. He requested an opportunity to address the review board when they met the following week.

II. ELECTIVE SURGERY

I have asked Dr. Nelrod to present me to you today so that I can describe the operation I have devised for you to perform. You spoke uneasily about death last week. You may leave the experience of dying to me, and simply do as you are asked to do. It will not be very different from what you have done before. You will be tempted to spare me pain, but pain will be my information as to what you are doing to me. You will be tempted to console me, but please resist the temptation. My consolation will be that the principles of my dying will become tangible to me as I investigate death. My only anesthetic will be my attention focusing on death as it enters a plane among other observables. As I die, I will feel the principles of my dying that will not themselves ever die. Your task will be to operate so precisely that I can correlate the pain I feel with what I know you to be doing. You will have to work quickly with clamps to stop bleeding, and perhaps keep up continuous transfusions of blood so that I do not lose consciousness of pain and become confused as to where I am and what is happening. You can decide on these details and assign tasks according to your skills. One of you should start with a foot and amputate the toes one by one. After one foot, I will be ready for a hand and a foot—fingers and toes to be amputated simultaneously and symmetrically. Perhaps a metronome could be used to establish a rhythm, so that the information in the pain is not distorted by noise. The relation between amputations of fingers and toes should, I think, be harmonic, and then the fingers of the other hand can be cut off as a reprise of the first foot, in order to allow my attention to recompose itself upon the familiar pattern. You will cut at the joints, guided by X-ray photographs which I will study with you, so that I, as the territory, will know the map that is guiding you into the territory. I think that my ears should be amputated in unison, and then I want them held in front of my eyes so that I can see into them. I suppose my hair will have been shaved off before beginning, and I consent to any other routine operating procedures except injections of chemicals to tranquilize me. The order of the next section requires more thought, and I am open to suggestion. Without fingers, I might still be tempted to raise my arms against you, even though they are restrained. Perhaps it is best not to cut at the wrists or elbows, but to have two of you work on my arms simultaneously from the shoulders, while one of you performs an orchiotomy. Since an orchiotomy is emotionally confusing, I intend to discuss it with a psychiatrist. I would like to experience the decisive acts of the operation without the effects of some archaic or infantile unincisive feelings. Perhaps my teeth should be removed earlier, in a separate operation; this will give me a chance to practice understanding pain. Other details will decide themselves. I think that my nose can go quickly, but that I will want to keep my tongue. I might want to say something; or moving it might help me to think. I cannot decide about my eyes. I am afraid that if they are cut out too soon, my attention will be thrown back upon my feelings and I will forget what you are doing to me. Yet the lack of eyes might help me to concentrate. You might simply cut the ciliary muscles, and if I like the effect on my focus we can leave it at that; and if I do not like it, we can completely remove the eyes. I am tempted to retain precise sight of you and your scalpels, but the attempt to correlate what I see you doing with what I feel you doing and with what I know you to be doing might be too difficult. Perhaps we should improvise at the time. I am undecided about some further details, such as an abdominal incision to permit removal of kidneys and liver, parts that might, like the corneas, usefully be transplanted into another body. I am indifferent on this point, and give you permission to do whatever serves your purposes. In conclusion, let me visualize myself for you, lying on the operating table—a head and a torso. I will need time to think, to formulate ideas and refine feelings. I may want to sleep, to consult the images in my dreams. I want to see the story my unconscious will come up with. When I wake, you will have withdrawn, for I will want to be left alone to feel my attention contract upon itself, and to know how it feels to witness my own death. You will excuse me now. I must rehearse that dream until it is strong enough to hold me in sleep so that I do not awaken to die too soon.

[21]

III.

FIRST REHEARSAL

Old man advancing toward me with an ax in his hand. The ax isn't an ax, it is a piece of metal twisted into cuneiform letters that spell Leonardo. In his other hand he holds a block of wood with the bark chopped off. I run into another room, and as I open a door, the doorknob comes off in my hand. I throw it to the ceiling where it becomes a crystal pendulum oscillating among lines of light. I close my eyes, and as I think I hear a slow approach, I see the interior of my eye and the web of blood vessels, and then I turn and walk backwards as shapes dilate ahead of me and contract behind me. In the wall approaching behind me there is a triangular hole. I reach toward it, and my hand is a wedge, but it doesn't fit the hole, which changes angles when I touch it. I feel heavier, my movement slows, yet with a last deliberate gesture I take off my hand, and with the stump of my arm I wedge the tetrahedronal hand into the rift in the wall. An edge of silence cuts across an edge of immobility. Stillness moves back and forth across me like a blade.

SECOND REHEARSAL

I float on the surface of the sea and watch waves unfurling upon each other. I know that hope will be the theme of the images, and then I worry that if the interpretation of the image in the dream is part of the dream, the interpretation will be only another image. I see myself as white—white as the blossom of a wave breaking against another wave. The bubbles look like letters of the alphabet, but as I strain to read what is there, I am looking at letters chalked on a

blackboard which is reflected in a trembling mirror mounted on the door of an armoire. With each movement of the door the words on the blackboard waver, and then I am in a strategy room and as officer-of-the-day I answer the telephone. A voice says, "Are you the party that called about the universal? I was told to tell you that we hadn't got anything for you today."

Third Rehearsal

A prison cell. I take a caramel candy out of my sleeve and unwrap it. I chew the candy and my teeth come out in the caramel. I look around to see that no one is looking and toss the wad of caramel and teeth onto the window sill. They become a pack of matches. I strike a match and hold it to my finger, which lights up with flame the color of caramel. I touch the walls and floor, which burn softly, and then my feet, and wherever I touch, a soft caramel flame spreads across the surface. My hands are in flames. I try to beat out the flames on my chest, but the movement only spreads the fire, and it hurts when a blue tattoo of flame unrolls across my chest and down my thighs.

Fourth Rehearsal

I lean on my elbow in bed and wonder if I have the courage to tell the doctors that the operation is a mistake. I lie back and raise my arm into the air to stretch, and then I see that it has been amputated from the shoulder. Have they operated without telling me? Perhaps they have cut off an arm as a preliminary to inure me. The refrigerator in the nurses' station shakes and then stops droning. I hear from

[23]

the radio a message that the bridge has been washed out, and then I hear a theme from *Carmen*. I want to wake up, but first I go acoss town to the customs office where I complain that an opera has been allowed to cross the border. Then Leonardo is trying to get into this dream, and I am flipping through the pages of his notebooks, more and more quickly, until the flickering pages form a motion picture of me lying in my hospital bed reading the last page of *Anna Karenina*. As I read Levin saying, "It is a secret, necessary and important for me alone and inexpressible in words," an old Italian man who was admitted to the hospital at the same time that I was, his wife screaming *per esperimentare, per esperimentare*, stands on the threshold of his room across the corridor from mine and touching the hem of his hospital gown shits on the floor. The word I have been looking for swims in my eyes too late: cherish. I should have found some way to keep my father warm in the barn. I want to escape from this dream unrecognized. Dejection.

FIFTH REHEARSAL

I slit open an envelope and read a letter that says, "The operation was unnecessary. It was possible until you had it and now it is no longer possible." Another letter: "You are dying, which would have been better under better circumstances. You could have done more than you did." I push the other envelopes off the bed and lie down, feeling not quite equal to the act of dying, but that I will approximate equality. Fifty-nine arrows fall to the ground. Each sound feels like an incision in my skin. Letters and words type themselves out in my mind, like when I learned to type, and I

think as I erase the letters that I can see what will never be said. The words to be spoken will remain possible because I will not speak them. The unspoken description of my dying will have to be imagined as something that could have been known although it will never be known. The meaning of my dying is what I would have said. I sit at the desk to write some letters. "Dear J., I think often of what you could have said but would not." "Dear K., I think often of what you could have said but did not." "Dear R., I think often of what you should have said but could not." "Dear T., I am sorry that what you might have said was usurped by silences and sibilant self-accusations."

IV. THE RESOLUTION

Everything that happens after I die continues the story of my life.

WOMEN

"An operation in mathematics is anything that leaves a scar."
                                          —TOBY SPISELMAN

How did you find me?

I connected points.

You're not supposed to know the recipient.

But the points connect into lines that converge on you, and now I have come to meet you.

You shouldn't upset me.

Am I upsetting you? Let me feel your pulse.

No, don't touch me. I don't like this visit. I didn't invite you. . . . What points did you connect?

Facts in the newspaper and my feelings. I allow my mother's heart to be transplanted into someone else's body, when I scarcely know what I am doing, after an accident which is less an automobile accident than murder and radical mastectomy—and now I must think about what I have done without thinking. Then the newspaper stories, the photographs, and the television interview: thirty-five-year-old pregnant divorcée receives heart in transplant operation. I had to wonder, as I tried to recover from my own experience in the recovery room at the hospital, where my mother's heart was, and whether or not she would approve what I had approved, just as you must wonder whose heart you have.

[26]

I haven't thought about her. I can't connect my life with your mother's life. And I have my little girl to care for. I don't dwell on the past, or on what might have been. I assume that your mother would be happy that her heart has helped someone.

That it's alive and well.

The dead must want the living to be happy. I must believe that, that I must be as happy as I can be for the sake of those who suffered, that I must be as alive as I can for the sake of the dead. I will not be guilty and unhappy because your mother is dead and I am alive. Is that what she would have wanted?

You could make me happy.

I can do nothing for you. You are angry and vengeful about your mother's death, but you agreed to donate the heart, and you have given up your rights in it.

Yes, it seemed legally mine to give, as I was being prepared for the operation on my chest. But don't say that you can do nothing for me. That is too extreme. It gives us both ideas.

Let me thank you for the heart, and then ask you please to leave me alone. I have my life, and I will not turn back to think about your mother, or turn aside to help you complete something with her that cannot be completed. The heart is only a pump, an impersonal muscle. You can rely on me to keep this heart alive as long as I can.

Isn't her heart keeping you alive?

It might have been anyone's heart.

Not just anyone died at the right moment in your preg-nancy for you to undergo such an operation.

[27]

Don't frighten me with what might have happened. My heart is beating so hard now that I can feel it thumping.

Let me see. I want to feel your pulse.

No, please, I must ask you to go away.

I'm not ready to leave. The heart which keeps you alive once kept me alive. You cannot deny our connection.

I don't know what you mean. I don't think like that.

I mean that I lived for nine months in my mother's body, and that my growth was paced by her heart. She and I overlapped, just as the lives of my daughter and me overlapped. If she and I overlapped before my birth, and you and she overlap after her death, then isn't there a region in which you and I overlap?

I live for myself and for my daughter, not for your mother or you.

I don't want the heart, I want you to have it. I feel better just seeing you. But I want to feel the connection between us. You feel the same systole and diastole that she felt. If I could hear your heart through a stethoscope, I could hear an amplification of her recurrences.

No, you would hear me, only me. The heart *is* as the heart *does*. I am not living on borrowed time with a borrowed heart, I am alive beyond the probabilities of life, and your mother is unfortunately dead. You can't hold a séance with her through me. I am only myself.

I like your strength, your resistance and your resilience. I can understand not wanting a strange woman to touch your heart.

There, you said it again, *your* heart. You admit that it's mine.

[28]

Yes, and you can let me touch you to feel it beating.

You're upsetting me on purpose.

You're blushing.

I am embarrassed. Surgeons held my heart in their hands. I don't know what they did with it, and I think that I don't want to know. Now you appear and demand some response that I wouldn't know how to give even if I wanted to.

She would have felt the same way.

Who?

My mother.

Damn your mother. I don't care what she would have felt. I am not the living dead.

She would have spoken like that, forcefully, but the words aren't true. You are not that isolated. Your life intersects her death and my heart. Your heart is our nexus.

You can't reach her through me, she's dead. Love her as she is, a woman who died. If you touch me, you touch me, and if you feel a heart beat, you feel my heart beat.

If I touch you. I will, and then we won't ask whose heart it is.

No, you're not going to touch me. I have an ugly scar.

Beautiful to me perhaps.

It's from the operation.

I'd like to see it.

No, you're frightening me with ghosts and fantasies.

Facts and true feelings might correct the fantasies. Let me touch your heart.

Will touching me convince you? That I am only myself? Here, put your hand here if that will satisfy you.

Where?

Here, on my chest.

Is this all right?

Yes, but I'm frightened now. Don't move your hand.

I can feel it. I feel your apprehension.

Are you satisfied now?

No, wait. I want to feel your pulse.

What are you doing?

There, that did it. I felt the response immediately, the change in your heart when I touched your hand.

Please, this is enough. You know that what you want is impossible.

No, only now do I know what I want, and that it is possible. I am not disappointed, only newly unsatisfied. Now I know the succession that my heart seeks.

Your heart?

Yes, my heart. I have one. It's beating rapidly now. I could feel faint, but I don't want to. Here, put your hand here, you can feel it for yourself.

Where?

Here, where the scar is.

MOTHERHOOD

As awkward as it is for me to write in defense of the operation that bears my name, I do so moved by the criticism that the operation is superficial because it is on the skin and for the sake of youthful beauty. I am aware that I was attracted to morphogenetic dermatology by the fact that few people died of skin disease. Perhaps that was cowardly of me, but suffering from pimples is suffering, and I have found that cures for the skin are often cures for unhappiness. I wasn't merely doing cosmetic surgery on the vain or the rich, and any cowardliness in becoming a dermatologist is more than offset by the courage of my operation. The criterion of beauty in science should also support my work, not because the operation restores physical beauty, but because the operation is beautiful in its elegance and simplicity.

While I don't ask for or expect the approval of physical scientists, I do think that their own self-interest would require them to support my work. For the object of my operation is not merely the amelioration of suffering caused by the disfigurements of aging, it is a proof of field as the principle of biological development. Before morphogenetic regeneration, field was either a metaphor from magnetism with no satisfactory operational definition, illustrated by photographs of iron filings, or field was a concept used by mathematical physicists to get rid of infinities which they could not tolerate in their equations. Now field can be defined operationally and is a concept that a child could understand.

I have in other places acknowledged Dreisch as the father of morphogenetic regeneration. His early work retains the freshness of a great discovery, and it lives encapsulated in the contribution it makes to the assumptions and procedures of our more sophisticated work. When Dreisch showed that a single cell from the embryo of a sea urchin would grow into another embryo, he was dry and factual at first, but gradually he realized that a few facts about morphogenesis destroyed deterministic theories, which were based on the picture of the growth of crystals. Deterministic theories collapsed when it was shown that a cell could develop along any one of many paths. The morphogenetic field is the total of such paths. The landscape in which the cell grows determines the path that it takes, and this landscape can be simulated in modern holographic medicine. The cell lives in a field of crisscrossed opportunities, and its development is guided by the opportunities open to it. Anyone who. has performed in a school laboratory the classical experiments on sea urchins and newts has seen the shaping power of the morphogenetic field.

Sea urchins and newts are less my problem than aging faces. I find no reason to think that aging is genetically determined. Genes do not provide information for the development of the individual beyond growth and the reproductive process in which the genes are transmitted to the next generation. Once past the reproductive stage, the individual has served the purposes of preservation of the species, and then he is on his own. The wrinkled human face is the victim of gravity and of cumulative errors in the reproduction of cells. Since aging is not programed, but is a badly improvised interference with youthful beauty, we have improvised an operation to counteract its effects. Aging is a form of misinformation. If we get the facts right, you will be able to read it in our faces.

I am not going to state for you the conclusions I have drawn about life while meditating on the faces I hold in my hand as I unwrap the bandages. I would rather describe the process of discovering the operation, which was almost accidental. I thought, while studying the faces of aging men and women, and while studying the science of morphogenetic development, that it might be possible to regenerate the human face. I was thinking of using templates made in youth to reorganize the cells of the sagging face into their earlier configurations. Toward this end, I was making templates of the morphogenetic fields of the faces of young women. We now know that such reversibility is impossible, and that the correct solution is, as it had to be, the simplest.

In thinking about the possible regeneration of faces, and in reasoning about embryology, I feared that I was dividing my attention, but then I could feel my separate interests converging toward a solution, as though guided by the undiscovered idea toward the idea itself. I knew I was near a solution without knowing what it was, and I had only to look into the eyes of a thirty-nine-year-old woman patient who chanced to be in my office—her ostensible problem a large naevus, but with two other problems—a wrinkled face and an unwanted pregnancy—and I saw the combination of my two interests and her two problems into a single solution: to use the cells from her embryo to regenerate her face.

When that moment returns to memory, I feel the idea hit me with the force of a physical object. The solution I had been looking for had found me. The operation had only to be seen there where it already existed as an objective possibility, although perhaps I had constructed my path toward the discovery by preparations which I had unwittingly made. My pleasure in the discovery is enhanced by the fact that I was not thinking about science or fame at that moment, I was simply feeling compassionate toward my patient.

I was not ready to operate on her. I diagnosed a shortage of zinc and referred her for collagen therapy. Then I took a leave of absence from the hospital and set up an abortion clinic on a Caribbean island where the religion was opposed to abortion, the government indifferent, and the natives quite ready to supplement their magic with free health care. I had to learn, by trial and error, the appropriate moment in pregnancy to ablate the fetus, to shred it into a sterile nutritive medium in which the cells could grow, and then to transplant the growing cells into the face which had been prepared by removal of the epidermis and dermal fat. At the present stage in the successful development of our operation, the last problem is credibility—a forty-year-old woman returns from a Caribbean holiday with skin like that of a child.

In theory the use of the fetus should be possible for the father as well as the mother, but the theory hasn't worked out so well in practice. In the native population, where it was sometimes difficult to identify the biological father, the problem was to be expected, but the same difficulty has been encountered with white American fathers. There may be a hormonal problem in the father that does not arise in the mother because of changes owing to pregnancy. These are difficult problems, but I like to say that our problems are more valuable than most doctors' solutions.

The attempt to use the fetus on the face of someone in the family beside the mother has usually failed. The causes are not known. It is awkward to have an occasional inexplicable success, such as we have had with two grandmothers and three maternal aunts. In one of our most interesting cases, the fetus from a twin was used successfully on the patient and her twin sister, who looked even more alike after the operation.

There has been criticism that women have become pregnant in order to have the operation. The best answer to this charge is to admit it. Yes, they have. The practice is justified because of the need to schedule the operation so soon after conception. Certain knowledge of the time of conception is important. Mistakes were made until this point was understood, and anything that helps to establish the precise time is justified.

The charge that I have played a role in these conceptions I will not dignify with a reply. These charges are diversions by the entelechists who will say anything to discredit my work. At least they do not underestimate its importance as a refutation of teleology. My relation to my patients is professional, although paternal. A positive attitude in the patient toward herself is therapeutic, and a fatherly air of approval is good medicine.

The woman who undergoes this operation can sense the morphogenetic field at work in her face. She can feel the lines of force as they guide the embryonic cells into the patterns they must form. Why should a woman let her life be determined by tired collagens or by a shortage of zinc which weakens her electromagnetic field, the matrix of life? The goal of life is living. Life is a field of opportunity, guiding the individual forward along paths created by the meshed forces of objective possibilities as they interweave with a person's own potentialities. And this philosophy of life is now bodied forth in the faces of beautiful women.

FATHERHOOD

I can't agree that the operation was as impossible as my colleagues now say. None of the objections is medical or biological, all are merely psychological, if not psychopathic. In no sense did the operation fail except that no donors were forthcoming.

The history of the operation is simple. Early work in the generation of one animal from the embryo of another by immersion in the morphogenetic field led to the possibility of regeneration of a human limb by creating a simulation of the morphogenetic field of the limb, a mesh of forces which would guide cellular development to construct an arm or a leg. If the first attempts were crude, later improvements in morphogenetic holography enabled doctors to regenerate arms or legs which were, through four-dimensional reversal, identical with the existing arm or leg which provided the template of the holographic field. The result was a greater bilateral symmetry than is possible in ordinary unsophisticated growth, and an unexpected dividend. The increased symmetry in children, subtle as it might seem, has resulted in different bodily experiences, and therefore in different feelings for symmetry in imaginative constructions. This so-called Dirac effect is yielding novel intuitions in particle physics and in zygotic algebra, for symmetrical scientists now define the evolution of the cosmos and the evolution of life both as a chain reaction of seriatim asymmetries. There is reason to hope that a mathematically gifted physicist, with regenerated and therefore symmetrical arms and legs, could achieve a unifield theory. Matter and energy may yet be understood as successive asymmetries of primal symmetrical space.

The benefits of the operation have appeared in topological mythography, where one of our own patients has recently demonstrated that as the myths of North America are to the myths of South America, and the myths of Europe are to Africa, so are the myths of North America to the myths of Africa, and the myths of South America to the myths of Europe. The beautiful result of these isomorphisms is that all these myths and their interrelations can be mapped onto the Chino-Indian myth of Kuan Yin, a process which clarifies the shaping forces of our society. Advances almost as important have been made in psychology, where feelings, now defined as vectors, have yielded to description in a scalar-tensor notation. If the direction and force of feelings can be altered, perhaps I will have a donor yet.

My operation may have lacked something in original genius, but it had, and still has, some creative daring. The plain fact is that more boys are born without penises, or lose the penis as the result of a burn during circumcision, or as an accident of war, than is publicly admitted or popularly realized. The solutions are grotesque: to rear the infant boy as a girl, with virtuoso operations, injections of hormones, the danger of siloxanic poisoning, and rarely the possibility of orgasm or pregnancy. Such phantom women haunt the halls of medicine, and their existence may satisfy some doctors who, suffering vicarious death so often, might long for vicarious life. But the operations are a farce. The doctors who create such hybrids should take a good look at themselves and at their irrational fear of holographic regeneration.

The operation for the regeneration of a penis could not work with holographic reproduction of the morphogenetic field, for the organ was missing and could not provide the template. Yet the powers of regeneration have been discovered to be so strong, and the importance of the penis to manhood is so obvious, that an operation had to be invented.

The first solution, certainly not my suggestion, was to make the holographic field plates from the father. This was of course a narrow and reductivist conception of a biomorphic field and the first operations were butchery, with the child fitted to the templates of his father's field, and his hopes, if he were old enough to understand, raised only to be disappointed. The field of one individual cannot be grafted onto the field of another. The idea of a field transplant derives from a failure to comprehend field. Every problem of medicine is a problem of language, and this operation was a malapropism.

My solution was, and I still say is, classical and elegant. The simple operation entailed only the transplant of the organ of the father onto the son, after making holographic field templates of the father, and then regenerating a penis not on the child, who would then have his father's penis, but on the father-donor. All the father has to give his son is his

FATHERHOOD

penis and a few months of his time while he grows a new
one. Such regeneration presents no difficulties, as we have
shown with adult males such as soldiers who have prov-
identially pre-filed the templates of their morphogenetic
fields. The only failure occurs when there is some tampering
with the field, as in the warpings of old templates. The plates
for the father-son operation would be fresh, since they would
be made immediately prior to the operation.

I will not write defensively about this operation. My theory
needs no defense, and my successful practice in generating
arms and legs speaks for itself. The onus, if there is any, lies
on those fathers who are asked to participate in an operation
which has many beneficial side-effects for themselves. If
anyone but the father could be the donor, medical authorities
would be indifferent, but the chances for rejection of the
transplanted organ are too great. The complaint that the regenerated penis would not be circumcised is trivial and un-
worthy in discussion of an operation devised to relieve great
suffering.

I do not think it too much to assume that, just as symmetrical mathematicians have different experiences of bodily
geometry, and have mapped the bone-space of the body onto
physical space with beautiful practical and theoretical results, so the son of a father who had donated his penis to him
would have different bodily experiences, and a different
genital space as a clue to the structure of existence, even as
he would have living proof of his father's vectors. The per-
plexing implications are there, waiting for psychologists to
unfold them. Think what might have been thought by the
mind of Sigmund Freud who either had the transplanted

[40]

penis of his father or who had made this gift to the manhood of his son. And think also of the pathos of the fact that we shall never know what could be felt by a son who had been made a gift of his father's penis, or for that matter, what could be felt by the father who made the gift and grew a new one.

DESIRE

La grande douleur de l'homme, qui commence dès l'enfance et se poursuit jusque à la mort, c'est que regarder et manger sont deux opérations différentes. La béatitude éternelle est un état où regarder c'est manger.
—SIMONE WEIL, "Contradiction,"
La Pesanteur et la Grace

Turning and climbing, the double helix evolved to an operation which had always existed as a possibility for mankind, the eating of light. The appetite for light was ancient. Light had been eaten metaphorically in ritual transubstantiations. Poets had declared that to be is to be a variable of light, that this peach, and even this persimmon, is light. But the peach which mediated between light and the appetite for light interfered with the taste of light, and obscured the appetite it aroused.

The appetite for actual light was at first appeased by symbols. But the simple instruction, promulgated during the Primordification, to taste the source of the food in the food, led to the ability to eat light. Out of the attempt to taste sources came the ability to detect unpleasant chemicals. These had to be omitted. Eaters learned to taste the animal in the meat, and the animal's food and drink, and to taste the waters and sugars in the melon. The discriminations grew finer—children learned to eat the qualities of the pear as they ate its flesh, and to taste its slow ripening in autumn sunlight. In the ripeness of the orange they recapitulated the history of the orange. Two results occurred. First, the children were quick to surpass the adults, and with their unspoiled tastes, and their desire for light, they learned the flavor of the soil in which the blueberry grew, and the salty sweetness of the plankton in the sea trout, but they also became attentive to the taste of sunlight. Soon there were attempts to keep fruit of certain vintages: the pears of a superbly comfortable autumn in Anjou, or the oranges of Seville from a year so seasonless that their modulations of bouquet were unsurpassed for decades. Fruit was eaten as a retrospective of light. Second, children of each new generation grew more clearly, until children were shaped as correctly as crystals. The laws governing the operations of growth shone through their perfect exemplification. Life became intellectually transparent.

The principles of growth, so obviously systematic, had seemed to emerge inexplicably from random change. The achievements of the species in development were attributed to chance. But this explained nothing more than that there was to be no further attempt at explanation. This theory, which saw chance provoking life into an empty future, was opposed by a theory which posited a principle mysteriously and progressively manifesting itself in the advances of evolution. The partisans of chance studied random distributions. The vitalists praised the life force.

But after several generations had supplemented their diet of flesh and fruit with light, and had experienced accelerations of evolution, the correct principle became self-evident: that evolution propels itself by an inclination toward its next probable achievement.

Evolution had been read with the influence either from the

past or from compresent relationships, neither of which ac-
counted either for the direction of change or for the stability
of the emergent level of achievement. The truth is that the
determining influence in evolution is from the possible future
toward which the population turns, guided not by chance
but by real future probabilities. The energy for movement
into the future is potential energy, deriving from the present
position relative to the force of the future probability. The
probabilities are of different degrees, and these differentials
constitute the gradients that shape the field. Evolution in-
clines toward probabilities.

No one could have known, as mankind entered a future
guided by the future open to it, that man would have the
opportunity to eat light. As the double helix turned, and
turned again, the eyes enlarged, the stomach contracted. As
some organs became vestigial, others transformed their functions, and the eye resumed some tasks it had abandoned
early in its phyletic past. The optic nerve tract expanded and
reached directly into the hypothalamous and the hypophysis,
with the effects on skin pigmentation which we are familiar
with. The body revealed unsuspected potentialities for photo-
synthetic functions, and we certainly can appreciate the way
the appendix adapted to purposes which had no precedent
in phylogeny. Such changes were speeded up when the principle of the voluble helix was understood. Then the future
probabilities could be simulated in a field of present probability functions, and several generations of development
could be compressed in an embryo grown within the field.
This very speedup, or spiraling, had a further accelerating
effect; and, in ways not well understood, the effect modified

the cause, for modifications of the gastrointestinal and optic systems modified the message of the DNA molecules. The key could stay the same, yet find that it worked in a different lock. These microscopic effects in genetics have been the model for the experiments on the total future. With our present comprehension of the macroscopic future as probabilities real enough to put a strain on the present, we are able to modify the present in order to develop leanings toward a desirable probability. We can, if we so desire, choose our communal future.

If we read now that an early people ate each other with their eyes, we of course misinterpret the relationship. They could not, as we do, eat the light reflected from another person, nor taste the colors of the beloved. The early appetite for light is difficult to understand, based as it is on no experience, and necessarily more frustrating than satisfying. Their comprehension of themselves as thickenings of light was sometimes advanced, although marred by guilt at interfering with the light. The taste for water, attested to in the literature, has been convincingly explained as a metaphor of the thirst for light. We may regard water as proto-light.

Yet, too, one must note the possible advantages for early man if he had been able to eat the light reflected from others. From the specimens preserved cryogenically, we see the array of colors from black and brown through pink. Delicious people. It is as though all possible shades were achieved within these colors, and there is evidence that we would have had much to envy, and much to eat, in the reflection from a young person. No wonder that the viewing of cryogenic bodies is limited to scientists.

DESIRE

Today, and let us celebrate this fact, we can eat the light of our beloved, warmed by compassion or cooled by intellectual feeling. And if we are surprised, and some of us disappointed, that the light is now only green—well, such was the vital probability awaiting us. We have, after all, an increase in the energy available for further evolution; we can use the energy of our position relative to the probabilities in the future to reach the future we desire. The full use of this energy is just beginning to be explored, and we have the opportunity open to few generations to create our best opportunities. We must not slacken in our desire now if we desire a future. The pressure of probabilities on the present increases the momentum of evolution, and as the voluble helix turns, and turns us away from our improbable satiation, we can see that the shadow cast on the present from the future is not black but rainbowed, brilliant with lemon-yellow, plum-purple, and cherry-red. I have no patience with those who say that their desire for light is satisfied. Or that they are bored. I have myself a still unsatisfied appetite for green: eucalyptus, celadon, tourmaline, and apple.

AMERICA: THREE AUDIENCES

I.

Professor Baluster: Good evening, Parents. We have been chosen to speak to you tonight as man and woman, as husband and wife, and especially as parents of neotenic twins, Salathial and Priscilla. Those of you who are having problems with only one neotene can imagine the problems we are having. We are also geneticists, my wife, Dr. Baluster, specializing in medical paedomorphology, a rapidly changing discipline which can be defined—she'll want to correct me, I'm sure—as the study of changes in the direction of evolution caused by neoteny, that is, when a physically immature stage of development such as a larva becomes capable of sexual reproduction. Since I study changes in evolution which result from changes in adult forms, or gerontomorphology, I'm not an expert on neoteny, at least not yet, but then I'm learning about it in my own home, as you are in yours. Dr. Baluster and I are surprised and gratified that our family experience is professionally useful. Because however you feel about neoteny, it must be said that the further we evolve into the future, the further we see into our phylogenetic past, and we can now confidently trace our evolution through the tunicates. More of that later. Let me say a few words about neoteny, and then my wife will speak on the practical problems of caring for the neotenic child, and we'll both be happy to answer questions.

Parent: I want to ask right now if there's some way my boy could be fixed.

Professor Baluster: Let's wait for the questions, please, but I'll answer yours since you've brought it up. The scientific and medical answer is yes, but the legal answer is no. Courts have ruled against sterilization of the neotene, and against involuntary birth control, and in fact against anything done without consent, which of course the child is too young legally to give. The age of consent would have to be changed.

Parent: My daughter changed it for herself.

Professor Baluster: I meant consent to the operation.

Parent: If prenatal tests indicate neoteny, is abortion possible?

Professor Baluster: Could we please wait on the questions? But since you've asked, the answer is that neoteny is detectable in the male but not the female neotenic fetus, and not with certainty, before the fifth month. I can say that Dr. Baluster has detected neoteny from concentrations of hormones in the amniotic fluid, and the chromosomal team here at Stratton Hospital is developing cytological examination of the karyotype. But no test is certain, and let me add—and I think I can speak for all of us—that our purpose is to advance science and to enhance human life, not to provide information for medical decisions on abortion. Neotenes reveal one of the possibilities of life, and are an achievement of evolution that must be revered, not a mere throwback.

Parent: There's nothing we can do about them?

Professor Baluster: No, and I hope you won't want to after our talk this evening. I should add that the neotenic fetus is precociously motile, and a motile neotene is a viable neotene. The rights of the viable fetus have been upheld in the courts.

Parent: What are we to do?

Professor Baluster: I can see that I'm not going to get through my talk, which was intended to anticipate many of your questions. We do think you should understand, so that you can accept the condition of your children, which is, after all, an acceptance urged on us by the probability that this wave of neoteny will be an irresistible tidal wave within a generation.

Parent: Isn't there a solution to this problem?

Professor Baluster: I think my wife might answer some of these practical questions which cause anxiety, and then we can explain the theory of neoteny later.

Dr. Baluster: I would like to join my husband in emphasizing the importance of a theoretical understanding to one's relations with the neotenic child. Certainly our work in biology and medicine has helped us, and I won't conceal from you that we parents need help, perhaps more so than do the children. But I think the best advice I can give you, which comes from my experience as a wife and mother, is simply this: Love the child, for what the neotenic child needs above all is love. Now you may think that all children need love, and that these children are difficult to love, as painful as it is for parents to admit that.

Parent: Don't you think they get enough love?

Dr. Baluster: No, I don't, not as I understand love, and am

qualified as a doctor to speak of it. Care for these children the way you would care for any child. Expect the children to be difficult. The expected will be easier to handle than the unexpected. Understand that their feelings are as impetuous as those of any child—they want what they want when they want it, and they don't like to wait. They know they don't have much time. We know how frustration leads to an impulse to aggression, and we don't want aggressive neotenic children. And we know how the frustration of aggression leads to depression, and we don't want depressed neotenic children either. So our only choice is the right choice, to give them their way, and to love them for their sakes as well as for our own, for the more difficult they are to love, the more we grow emotionally in loving them. My husband and I say that loving our neotenes has been an educational experience, for we have learned not only that we need to give love, but that the more difficult the love is to give, the purer the love is. When the object of love is difficult, as the neotenic child admittedly can be difficult, then the love of the child can be constructed as consciously and as rationally as a scientific experiment, and the love can be seen as an ideal structure that is what we choose it to be, without the convections caused by external forces. Our children have taught us about ourselves. Some of the lessons have been painful and some delightful, but the whole has been an education in the experience of theorized love.

Parent: An education in licentiousness.

Dr. Baluster: Only if you choose to think of it that way. The experience does have its shocking aspects, but you will get used to those. And remember the darkness in their lives, a fact you might prefer not to think about, but which—if you can face it—will help you to give them the love they need for healthy growth. Then you will comfort yourselves when they are gone with the knowledge that you did everything you could have done. Neotenes die at twelve, thirteen or fourteen years of age, and they know it. We could not, even if we wanted to, keep the knowledge of their deaths from them. If you don't tell your children about death, others will, and it is better that they learn it from you, if only because you will teach yourselves about it in the process of teaching them. You will be suprised by their attitude, I think. They see no purpose in living beyond thirteen or fourteen, and their games and little songs reconcile them to early death.

Parent: We know their games well enough.

Dr. Baluster: I know that you are angry about their sexuality and their deaths. You will have to learn to accept the fact that you can't control their sexual development, which might make you feel anger, and that you can't control the fact that they are going to die, which might make you angrier still.

Parent: I just don't like any of it.

Dr. Baluster: All the more reason to use this experience, for in learning about neotenes, we can learn something about our latent selves. They are not gnomes so much as they are gnomons. But always they are children, and what they do is neither right nor wrong, it is natural. Their sense of time is adjusted to their span of life, so that a year of their lives is like six or seven of our years, and an act which seems short to us seems long to them. We cannot judge the quality of their lives. The genesis of their ideas of time, space and causality is fascinating, and a genetic psychologist will speak to us another evening on the world of the neotene, a charming talk called "Kant and Piaget in Lilliput." But don't let me get ahead of myself. Let me return to my point, which is that these apparently abnormal children are the norm of the future. Enjoy them while they are lent to you. Care for them. Love them so that they do not enter and depart this world without love. No one should suffer that deprivation.

Parent: What about their children?

Dr. Baluster: Yes, we will be young grandparents. Some of us are already, and while this transition from adult to infant sexuality occurs, and we witness a privileged moment in evolution, we can look forward to being grandparents and to having even more children to love. I say that love isn't like a pie, that if you give a piece to six people you'll have none for a seventh. Love is like a muscle, and the more you use it the stronger it grows. Which reminds me, some of you parents might want to discuss the effect of neotenes in the household on your own sexual feelings.

Parent: Some of us just might not want to also, Lady.

Dr. Baluster: As you will. But frankness about these problems is helpful to everyone. And now, while we are speaking primarily of neotenes tonight, I want to say a word about neuters, because some of you may be parents of both neotenes and neuters, or your neotenes might give birth to neuters. Count yourself fortunate in either case. The parents of neuters will have the comfort of knowing that, if they are not able to, the neuters will be capable guardians of their neotenic children. We may feel that no one could bring up our children as well as we do, but I can assure you that neuters do a superbly efficient job. Are there other questions?

Parent: Incest.

Dr. Baluster: Do you know we had a symposium on incest recently, and we're defining the problem. Most peoples have banned marriage between siblings and between certain other kin, but they certainly didn't control, and many didn't ban, sexual relations. You may remember some incestuous sexual play from your own childhoods. Now since neotenes are too young for marriage, they really don't fall under the taboo against the marriage of siblings, and we as biologists and physicians see no reason to forbid intercourse between siblings. It would interfere with the possible mutation of new forms, and would be eugenics with no scientific principles to guide it. Some of the children are born blind or dwarfed, but we must accept them, for they reveal the possibilities in the genetic pool, and teach us even more about life.

Parent: What do we do about incest, then?

Dr. Baluster: You do nothing because there is nothing to do. Any rules to repress their activity have the opposite effect. You would only be putting ideas into their heads. Learn to live with it. Parents of brother-sister neotenes who have ever tried to separate them will know why I say that.

Parent: Why do they die so young?

Dr. Baluster: The truthful answer to that question is that we do not know. After all, they have matured sexually and been able to reproduce, and have thereby satisfied one of the purposes of life. But I am not sure that the cause is either metabolic or psychogenic. I suspect that the cause is an intellectual discovery which they make about their biological

growth. I have watched the neotenic child start to die at the
discovery of the contradiction between feelings of irreversible
physical change in the body and feelings of reversible logical
operations in the intellect. The neotene does not die so much
as suffer an annulment of life at the convergence of the reversible and the irreversible.

Professor Baluster: These early deaths are sad, no doubt,
but my wife and I want to leave you with a positive impres-
sion of the parenthood of neotenes. It would help if you understood how strictly determined this development is, and on
another evening I will deliver a talk I have prepared, "A
Dextrous and Dextrorse Helix." Understanding might help to
change your attitude, which you must change if only because it is all that you *can* change. Consider yourselves lucky.
Parents of neotenes are in the future now, and posterity will
look back on us with gratitude because we found traces of the
future in the present and fostered them.

Parent: Protected them.

Parent: Nurtured them.

Parent: Encouraged them.

Dr. Baluster: Anomalous curvatures in the electromagnetic
field of the body are amplified into feelings such as love of
beauty or of children. Do not shrink from love of these beautiful children who hurl themselves toward us, for they are
irresistible waves unfurling from irreversible tomorrows.

II.

"With rapid sketches on the board, [Walter Garstang]
made a brilliant survey of the larvae of many different
groups and showed how in each there is a compromise
and adjustment between two rival needs—or in other

words, two competing selective advantages: on the one
hand to grow up as soon as possible so as to reproduce
the species, and on the other to remain floating as long
as possible so as to distribute the species over the largest
areas."

—SIR ALISTER HARDY,
The Open Sea, Boston, 1970

Neuters, I want in the remaining minutes to outline our
lectures. Whatever your feelings about the neotenes, suppress
them, but remember that we nurture the neotenes for the
Neuters they will bear. We depend upon these our depend-
ents. We must breed neotenes. You will find that they thrive
on our neglect. As you study paedogenesis, you will appreciate neotenes as living specimens for study. They are walking
biopsies. Our lectures on the evolution of Neuters will take
you back through the tunicates, the pelagic sessile inverte-
brates that sent up larvae which would descend elsewhere for
their sessile adult stage. The larvae gradually developed
gonads and began to reproduce themselves directly, without
descent to the adult stage. Further evolution of tunicates pro-
ceeds paedomorphically from larval forms, but the generation by those larval forms of sessile Ascidians has remained
a possibility in further evolution. Now the neotenes have
emerged as throwbacks to the free-floating sexually mature
larvae, and we Neuters are the modern realization of the
sedentary adult stage. The Larvacea developed into the
chordates and have brought us from the pelagic sea to this
laboratory. Since our evolutionary emergence depends upon
the neotenes, and we are sterile, we must not be indifferent
to them.

Every possible biological function or principle of operation exists in reserve until evoked by a novel concatenation of adenine, thymine, cytosine, or guanine. This reservoir of biotic possibilities is the evolutionary future. The origin of species is the seriatim succession of an unlimited sequence of principles of operation. Species are displaced not by the probabilities of population genetics, but because all possible principles of biological functioning have the energy to actualize themselves. Where does the energy for these advances in order come from? It derives from the future as a field of a transfinite number of point-instants. The farther point-instants can be assigned a very small probability value, since so little is known about them, and that probability value can be represented by a continuous curve, because what is infinitesimal to the abscissa will be infinitesimal to the ordinate. But the nearer point-instants, which can be assigned larger and more definite probability values, are difficult to plot as continuous curves. This difficulty in representation must not be allowed to obscure the fact that the probability is not merely represented by a curve, it *is* a curve, and above a certain threshold this curve becomes potential energy which disappears from the future and in a quantum jump appears in the present as kinetic energy. At the same time, kinetic energy in the present disappears and reappears in the future as modifications of a probability curve. This energy from the future enters experience, according to wave theory, as waves which pass on their curvature to present probabilities, intensifying them into actualization. And of course changes in the present spatio-temporal curvatures release waves which pass on their curvatures to the probabilities in the future. I may be getting too far ahead in our story, but I want you to grasp the symmetrical exchange of energies between present and future, and the fact that available energy is a constant. An increase in order or in probability is not a loss of available energy but the conservation of energy as potential in the curvature of probabilities. When you learn the rules for the transformation of probability curves into spatio-temporal curvatures, you will see how present and future energize each other in reciprocities faster than the speed of light.

I have gone too far ahead in the story, however. Some of you, six or seven years old, will prefer psychology to evolutionary physics. Psychological motivation is the desire to change relations between two points, and so psychology is the study of equations with two unbound variables. You will learn to assign values to these variables, and to plot these values as a curve that can be mapped onto probability curves. Psychology might motivate some of you less than physics, but you will be interested when you discover that the energies measured in physics are the motives felt in life, so that you can close the distance between motive and motion by constructing a physics of the emotions. Think of your feelings toward the neotenes. They would make interesting if comic physicists themselves, because the size of their bodies is wrong for the earth. They are not built to scale, like a toy, but are built as working models, with a peculiar relation of surface to mass to function that should yield a self-consistent but distorted geometry, with all curvatures warped by errors in the scale of skeletal and genital space. Amuse yourselves sometime by projecting with them the geometry of their experience. But take them seriously, for only then will they be truly entertaining. At the conclusion of the course, you can satisfy your curiosity about the anatomy of neotenes when you perform dissections and see what they are with your own eyes.

III.

"In adult man . . . the aperture of the vagina is directed ventrally. The human mode of copulation is therefore associated with the neotenous condition of the pubic region of the body."

—Sir Gavin de Beer,
Embryos and Ancestors, Oxford, 1972

Good morning, boys and girls!

Good morning, Miss Louise! Good morning! Good morning!

That's enough "good morning," now, children, or it will be afternoon. Guess what we're going to talk about this morning, boys and girls.

What Miss Louise, what? Tell us, tell us right now.

This morning, boys and girls, we're going to talk about *you*!

Us! About *us*! Oh goody!

Yes, and if you'll stop that a minute, Leon—you there, little boy, stop now.

I'm not so little, Miss Louise. Do you want to see?

No, no, Leon. Now let's all say "Good morning" to the boys and girls at home.

Hello, boys and girls, hello, hello, hello!

And now, boys and girls—please sit apart there, the way I showed you, or Miss Louise won't invite you back on her program—now we're going to talk about where babies come from.

They come from in here, Miss Louise, I'll show you. I've got one in there now, and it'll come out down here.

That's interesting, Kimberly, but that isn't quite the way it happens. Now suppose I ask about differences between you and me. Doreen?

You're flat-chested, Miss Louise? Is that it?

No, Doreen, let's hear what Tammy has to say.

Your eggs are old, Miss Louise, is that it? You have old ovums.

That's not what I was thinking of, Tammy. What do you think I was like when I was a child? Was I like you?

No, Miss Louise, I don't think so.

You're right, Josephine. Tell us how you think I was different.

You were a virgin, Miss Louise. Right?

Never mind now, Josephine. Children, let's say "Happy Birthday" to our friends at home who are having birthdays today. I look in the Magic Mirror, and my goodness, I see Brian and Harold, Happy Birthday, and Happy Birthday Kevin and Forrest and Nadine. And "Hello" and "Happy Birthday" to all the mommies who are watching with all you little neotenes.

My mommy is a neotene, Miss Louise, just like me.

That's nice, Shelley. Now what's another difference between you and me when I was your age? Dewayne? No ideas? Samantha?

You didn't like boys?

There's some truth to that, Samantha. Now, children, it's time to play a little game.

Can we play doctor, Miss Louise? We could play doctor.

See that white stuff I wiped on your dress, Miss Louise?

Ah, what is it, Leon? Get it off. What is it?

It's just glue, Miss Louise, just all-purpose glue.

Do you want to play Teacher! Teacher! Miss Louise?

No, Dewayne, I don't think I know that game. Roger, leave Kimberly alone. Doreen, you sit here beside Kimberly. Now we're going to play a game called "What in the World?"

Do you want to play with me, Miss Louise? I don't mind. I've done it with grownups.

You haven't any such thing. He hasn't, Miss Louise. He's lying.

Yes too I have.

Prove it!

I'll bet you a million dollars I have.

Children, children! We're going to play a different game, one that we haven't played before, a game that will teach us something about my world and your world. Don't sit on Doreen like that, Tammy. Children, get off each other. You there, stop it, get off!

I'm not going to do games, Miss Louise. I don't have time for no games.

Any. Ambrose, *any*. You don't have time for *any* games.

That's what I said, Miss Louise, and don't forget, I wouldn't do it with you, or even show you my whomper, because you're too old, you have lived too long, and you have too long to live.

MÉTIER: WHY I DON'T WRITE
LIKE FRANZ KAFKA

Do you think that she was writing about you?

No, not at all. It would be vanity to think so. The writer she describes is a master of illusion.

And you are the master of non-illusions?

You mean to be kind, but mastery itself is the illusion. You haven't touched that machine. Does it start itself?

Yes, it's voice-activated.

You should avoid attributive nouns. Don't use *voice* as an adverb, it's a noun. Do you mean that if I remain mute the machine will stop? That it won't record my silence?

It will for several seconds. It has a time-lag device.

Then I am afraid that your interview will misrepresent me if it elides my silences. Aside from silences, my speech consists chiefly of quotations, what Horatio Greenough complained of: "Extraneous and irrelevant forms invade that *silence* which alone is worthy of man when there is nothing to be said." Perhaps the machine will record the ruffle of pages as I look up quotations.

I would say that *voice-activated* is a compressed prepositional phrase, *by voice-activated tape recorder*. The *by* is silent.

[61]

If you are writing a thesis on my work, I hope that you write better than you speak. Did you know that the fifteenth-century mystery plays were mastery plays, performed by masters of a guild, men whose craft was a mystery? They must have felt that their work was authorized and added something. If you are going to know my books, you need to know what I know. That is why I have agreed to this interview.

I'm sorry that you resent this.

I haven't said that I resent anything. Don't interpret me to myself: wait until you get home and listen to the tape. You seem to think that you have something to say about my writing that the writing doesn't say, and I am eager to discover what it could be. Perhaps you will use your skills as a Master of Arts in Literature to teach me what I have been trying to learn about myself by writing. I have quoted Polanyi's words to explain my writing: "It is a systematic course in teaching myself to hold my own beliefs."

I think that you of all writers have avoided self-delusion. You seem to have more of the spirit of a scientist than a writer of fiction.

Don't try to delude me into thinking that I am a scientist. My work cannot succeed or fail like scientific work. I write fictions to prove falsehoods, which a scientist cannot do. I am envious. They have had the important moral experience of our time.

Do you mean the war?

No, the extent to which they have been able to conceal from themselves what they are doing, and the extent to which they have concealed themselves from themselves. They have risked being faithless to their experience, and have pretended not to notice the mystery in being where and what they are. Their belief has brought into observable existence a plane which is beyond the ken of most of us. Why should I read fiction when I can read Saccheri and Lambert attempting to prove the Euclidian axiom of parallels, and inadvertently proving theorems in non-Euclidian geometry? Or I read Galois, the letter he sat up to write the night before the duel in which he was killed, revising his mathematical discoveries. Twenty years old.

Have you used his theorems?

I might have, but Galois is beyond me. Even if I understand the argument, I do not understand the passion. I learn more from the discouragements of someone like Hermann Weyl, who was developing a geometry in which the length of the vector changes and then gave it up. I stopped mathematics because I did not understand what I was doing, and years later learned that I might not have needed to because I could not have known. Now the possibility of your interpretation tells me that I might not know what I have been writing, either, and I will have to decide whether or not that makes a difference. I suppose that one is a scientist *malgré lui*, the only question being whether he is a successful or an unsuccessful scientist, and I have associated myself with failed scientists in order to associate myself with failed irony, and in order to find the moments when appearances and experience successfully survive the interpretations that would annihilate them. Each failure of irony is the proof of an appearance. Are you interested in this?

Do you think that your work is in the tradition?

[63]

MÉTIER

Why do you change the subject? Which tradition?

I wonder who you see anticipating your work or influencing you.

My sources and analogues? I have a few touchstones. I write mental thank-you notes for certain passages, and then I mentally tear them up and collage the fragments into a story. The pieces don't fit together. Eight words from Shakespeare are one of my sources: "We two saw you four set on four. . . ." I am influenced by Alexander Pope, "And ten low words oft creep in one dull line." Wordsworth, of course, is an analogue: "I measured it from side to side, / T'was two feet long and three feet wide."

Are you serious?

I have just warned you against irony. I am telling you everything I can. Robert Frost, of course: "A cord of maple, four by four by eight. . . ." Listen to this sentence, so beautiful: "from left to right twenty-three, twenty-two, twenty-two, twenty-one, twenty-one, twenty, twenty-one, twenty, twenty." You recognize Robbe-Grillet. All the distortions of possessiveness are rendered in that sentence. The effects of jealously are conveyed by a man counting banana trees. Brilliant. I wish I had written such a line. I can give you more quotations so that you can make a mistake with them.

What do you expect me to do wrong?

I will be disappointed if you don't focus past the fragments I quote onto some theme, and credit me with a depth I don't have.

But what if I do see a unifying motif?

You think the mention of numbers has a meaning?

You can't deny that the numbers are a meaningful theme.

And you can't tell me what the numbers mean, so you certainly can't tell me what the mention of numbers means. Can you define a number, or tell me how it exists, or the differences between numbers and numerals, or between counting and ordering? The words for numbers are in a separate class from words that are the names of things. The names of numbers are like the names of feelings, like the feeling of whether or not one is alone, or is surrounded by just the right accumulation, or whether one is nothing. The names of certain numbers touch my feelings the way a cat returning to her nest of kittens with a bird is touched by the feeling of rightness or wrongness of her collection, or the way a bird returning to its nest feels presence and absence. Here, listen to Whitehead. You will think that I mentioned Galois before because Whitehead refers to him here, but I didn't know that I would need this passage. "Consider Ramanujan, the great Indian mathematician, whose early death was a loss to science analogous to that of Galois. It was said of him that each of the first hundred integers was his personal friend." And then Whitehead says that he cannot claim "intimate friendship" beyond one, two, three, four, and five. Beautiful, isn't it, the idea of intimate friendship with an integer.

You certainly can't expect me not to notice your use of numbers.

Have you counted them? Have you given each a number, and each number a name? I want you to notice that you don't have any idea what a number is the name of. So I will give you one idea. A number is the name of a feeling. Whitehead lived in England with his wife and a few children. Ramanujan was born in Madras. He wrote to G. H. Hardy, "I am now about twenty-three years of age," when he actually was twenty-five. Chaucer was casual when he said that he was "*quarante ans et plus*," but then he wasn't a friend of the first hundred integers.

Why do you suppose Ramanujan underestimated his age then?

He didn't estimate it. He gave the number closest to his age that is a prime number, and was the name of the feeling he had about himself. Hardy would understand that he had only himself and was alone among twentys, twenty-ones, twenty-twos, twenty-fours, twenty-fives, and was looking for someone with properties similar to his own. Most of us have lost the delicacy of feeling that would enable us to recognize the difference between feeling twenty-three, and divisible only by twenty-three or one, and feeling twenty-four, and divisible by two, four, six, eight, and twelve.

I think I feel something of your meaning, but I couldn't say what it is. Perhaps when I play back the tape I'll be able to follow better.

Then I shall say something for the machine now, to keep it activated, which will be there for you later when you are a voice-activated Master of Arts. You will eavesdrop on my conversation with your machine. As you join us, you hear me saying, My thoughts are windows, but please focus on the glass, not on the landscape that might be seen through the window.

Like a mirror?

No, you cannot look away from the fireplace to the window and see the flames reflected in the glass superimposed on the snow-covered trees outside and say, Oh the burning bush. I ask you to resist the temptation to see through my words, to look past what I am saying. Each story is written in a foreign language, and the meaning of the story is in learning how to read it.

I made a note to ask about the quotations from other languages.

Yes, I dislike quotations in foreign languages. I'm never certain that I have understood them. Why doesn't someone translating a novel from French translate the German quotations in the novel? I find that practice, as I find you, attractively irritating.

But you frequently quote other languages without translating. I've been assigning my students excercises in identifying and translating the quotations. There could be an annotated edition someday. But if they aren't important. . . .

They are indispensable signs to the reader that something uninterpretably alien approaches.

But the epigraphs. When I teach the stories, I find that the quotations, after I translate them, illuminate and amplify the themes.

What is true and what can be taught are separate investigations. Why should the stories be read the way you read them? The style in which the stories require to be read is the style in which experience is to be read. I taught myself to write in order to find the boundaries of my beliefs—to learn to read how I read existence.

Then what do the stories mirror?

Nothing. They are neither mirrors held up to nature, nor mirrors moving along a roadway, nor mirrors that reflect an infinite unity and then when smashed continue in each smallest fragment to reflect the same infinite unity. They are like shards of glass in a glazier's bin, the scraps that fall when a sheet of glass is cut to specifications. That's why I don't write like Franz Kafka.

Sir?

Please do not speak to me as *cher maître*. Let us confront our inequality and attempt to approximate equality as closely as we wish. Were you listening when I told you why I don't write like Franz Kafka or Sigmund Freud?

Perhaps I wasn't paying attention.

Perhaps I had not earned your attention. You know what Joyce wrote about Moses.

No, I know he was amused that his name and Freud's both mean *joy*, but I haven't studied Joyce.

Yet you would play upon me. But never mind. There was a trial, years before *Der Prozess*, of a man accused of fractricide. Joyce attended the trial and heard Seymour Bushe, a barrister, describe the *Moses* of Michelangelo. Joyce adapted the description in Ulysses: "That stony effigy, in frozen music, horned and terrible, of the human form divine, that eternal symbol of wisdom and prophecy which, if aught that the imagination or the hand of sculptor has wrought in marble of soultransfigured or of soultransfiguring deserves to live, deserves to live." You must have wondered why I don't write like Franz Kafka. You have read Freud on the *Moses* of Michelangelo?

In college, I think.

Perhaps you think Freud thought that he was Moses.

I haven't thought about it. Are you asking if I think Freud identified with Moses, or that he was deluded?

How could Freud have been deluded—the master of non-delusion? Could the author of a theory that uses the name of Oedipus for the feeling of desiring to kill the father himself kill the father of the Jews so that he could take his place and not know it?

I don't know enough to have an opinion.

I am telling you what I must know and what you must know to know what I know. What are the facts? Gombrich wrote, "If there is any work of art that the cultured Jews of Central Europe adopted, it is this vision of the Hebrew leader." Passionless. Vulgar. Passionless is vulgar. Adopting a work of art. "If there is any work of art, it is this vision. . . ." Sigmund Freud did not adopt a statue. He was capable of begetting his own art.

I thought that Freud. . . .

You thought, but you sat upon your thought and dreamed that you possessed something, when you should have walked the idea up and down. Freud first saw the statue of Moses in 1901. Quickly, you do not have much time. He wrote that he "expected Moses to start up at any moment." And in 1914 he wrote that Moses was in the act of sitting down.

Had anything happened to Freud to change his mind?

The change is in Moses. Jones says that Freud identified with Moses, "and was striving to emulate the victory over passions that Michaelangelo had depicted in his stupendous achievement." How lukewarm and flaccid, "stupendous achievement." Freud is using his authorship to make Moses

[69]

sit down. He was no *tyrannus*. Bakan says that Freud thinks Moses will not rise up and punish him. The son offends but the father does not punish. Bakan knows how to hurt. His Sigmund Freud asks to be let off with a light sentence or with no sentence at all for apostasy and patricide. As though Freud would have accepted mercy from Moses when the point is that Moses has no jurisdiction over him.

I have perhaps stayed too long today. I can return again when it is convenient.

It is convenient only now. You cannot escape the process you have begun so easily. You cannot activate my voice with this machine and then leave because I do not like your tepid questions. Freud was not easy on himself. What would he have asked me? Listen to him, he quotes the interpretations that disagree with his. Jacob Burckhardt, "Moses seems to be shown in that moment in which he catches sight of the worship of the Golden Calf, and is springing to his feet." And Springer, "Moses is about to start up in wrath." Even Hermann Grimm, "He sits there as if on the point of starting to his feet," and Heath Wilson, "he is about to leap to his feet, but is still hesitating." He quotes Lubke, Wölfflin and Justi against his argument. So he concludes the case after giving the arguments for the other side: "His lifted foot can hardly mean anything else but that he is preparing to spring up."

But I thought. . . .

Yes, you thought, but Freud saw. He could see Moses sitting down.

So Freud contradicted his earlier statement?

No, Freud contradicted Michelangelo's contradictions. He

quotes Max Sauerlandt, "No other work of art in the world has been judged so diversely as the Moses with the head of Pan. The mere interpretation of the figure has given rise to completely opposed views."

So it is ambiguous.

No, because the ambiguity is not ambiguous. Freud said it: "The artist is no less responsible than his interpreters for the obscurity which surrounds his work." Responsibility for obscurity is unambiguous. Freud saw Michelangelo and the biblical passage which he misinterpreted. . . .

Michelangelo misinterpreted?

My Dear, with each idea and image you take me back to the beginning where my ideas began, and I feel young and informative again. I am enjoying this interview. I find you charming because you fool me into thinking that I know something or that I have something to say. You are a demon of my self-infatuation. Haven't you been listening? Joyce called the statue "horned and terrible," and Sauerlandt wrote of it as the "Moses with the head of Pan." For centuries the halo of light was misunderstood as horns. "And the children of Israel saw the face of Moses, that the skin of Moses' face shone." "So sahen dann die Kinder Israel sein Angesicht an, dass die Haut seines Angesichts gläntzte." Joyce had it right, of course, "the light of inspiration shining in his countenance," and Kafka, "like a halo or a high mark of distinction," "wie ein Schmuck oder eine hohe Auszeichnung." Sometimes I think that Freud's Moses is the psychoanalyst who would like to get up, throw down his pad, and leave the patient alone in the room, but who overcomes the urge because he needs the patients performing their transferences onto him so that he can see how he is translated into their languages.

But Kafka? I thought you said. . . .

Kafka. I did. 1914. Kafka read the first chapter of *Der Prozess* to Max Brod. In December he finished the ninth chapter, and early in 1915 chapters five and six.

And Moses?

Moses. You think I lose the thread. 1914. Freud's essay on the *Moses* of Michelangelo. Joyce begins *Ulysses*. Kafka describes the Justice as he is painted in oils, about to "spring up with a violent and perhaps wrathful gesture," and a similar portrait in pastels, "Here too the Judge seemed to be on the point of rising menacingly from his high seat, bracing himself firmly on the arms of it."

It could be the *Moses*.

Could be. Could be. Wait until you hear yourself on this tape. Listen to the words. Kafka writes, *"als wolle er . . . aufspringen,"* and Freud quotes, *"als wollte er eben aufspringen,"* from Grimm, and *"Moses . . . aufspringen will"* from Burckhardt, and *"Moses . . . im Zorn aufspringen will"* from Springer. The Judges are painted in the posture of the statue of Moses when he seems to be about to spring up out of his chair.

Then Freud and Kafka disagree.

What if Freud writes that Moses is sitting down, and Kafka that he is springing up? Remember Kafka's words: "The right perception of any matter and a misunderstanding of the same matter do not wholly exclude each other."

I've wondered why he didn't finish and publish *The Trial*.

Because he was thinking about Moses, and if he wrote for

[72]

anyone other than himself—if he wrote some entertainment that someone might enjoy publishing so that others could enjoy reading—he would not be certain that he was thinking for himself.

But you have written that thinking is a social act and that philosophy and friendship are convertible. I have taught your story, "philosophy: a friendship in the Andes." You have written. . . .

I have written, I have written, but I am speaking of Kafka, not of what I have written. I want to know why I don't write like Franz Kafka, and you are wondering why he did not live his life as a bicycle stunt at the Variety Theater. You are making me forget what I wanted to say about Moses. What I wrote in that story is that truth is always and only a consensus. I meant it at the time. Freud and Kafka do not contradict each other in 1914 because each is thinking the same thought. It makes no difference whether Moses is sitting down or standing up, because Moses should no longer make a difference.

Why not?

Because they will be the source of their own law. They do not succeed to Moses. They do not accept their inheritance, and I inherit, not what they inherited, but their abrogation of their inheritance. I cannot disown them as they disowned Moses. Moses is zero to Freud and zero to Kafka. Zero equals zero. Freud wrote about love and death as "an equation with two unknown quantities." Freud and Kafka are my unknown quantities, like love and death, but they decide equally that Moses should not make such a difference to love and death. The Moses of Freud equals the Moses of Kafka as zero equals zero, a formula in which no substitutions can be made because it does not contain a variable. If we add the fact that Joseph K. is a land surveyor, a *Landvermesser*. . . .

But that is in *The Castle*, not *The Trial*, and he's merely K. there, not Joseph K.

Yes, there is a difference. How interesting you might have been. I don't know why you want to take my measure as a writer, but I am glad that I have explained to you that the only formula that can be derived from zero equals zero is the formula zero equals zero. I am glad I have given you the proof.

The proof?

I don't take umbrage at Moses, and I'm not going to take umbrage at you. I have given you the proof of the reasons why I don't write like Franz Kafka.

HISTORY: A STORY HAS ONLY A FEW GOOD YEARS

I.

John Wycliffe, 1380, and John Purvey, 1388, translating from I Corinthians XIII: And we seen now bi a myrour in derknesse, but thanne face to face; now Y knowe of parti, but thanne Y schal knowe, as Y am knowun.

II. 1900

FROST: Why did he think he wanted to climb among the glaciers?

FIRE: He heard that a party of explorers had discovered the fragment of a mountain forest carried along intact in the midst of glaciers. He wanted to see the picturesque scene, the island of trees grown together into a black roof over the sandy white forest floor. He wanted to touch the lichen on the rocks, to think about birch trees, to meditate on saxifrage and time.

FROST: He was in love.

FIRE: He thought about it. He wanted to see the rocks and peat supporting trees and flowers, and violets blooming against the edge of ice, their leaves translucent in cold light slicing from the glaciers.

[75]

FROST: He thought himself incapable of love.

FIRE: He had gazed at Althea adoringly until he realized that his life had stopped while he contemplated hers. She seemed to be resilience bodied forth as girlishness, and he hesitated between the words *sinuous* and *sinewy*. He had a feeling for the form of a poem that was filling itself in with words as he dismounted from the horse at the cabin and strode through the glare of the glacial field toward the cross section of ancient forest. Yet Dr. Colby had called him neurasthenic.

FROST: "I cannot take for wife,
A woman who is less than Life."

FIRE: The first revision:
"I will take for wife.
A woman who will heighten Life."

FROST: He should have been warned.

FIRE: No one had seen avalanches fall or heard crevices open in the night. No geologists knew the lakes of water that grew within the crowns of ice and then with one surge lifted the glacier, freezing as it flooded.

FROST: He wanted to be here for the New Year, January first, 1900, but feared the weather. He did not want to miss parties in the East. By November, leaves would congeal upon the trees.

FIRE: He found the date, June the sixth, in Byron, the sixth day of the sixth month, Don Juan, aged sixteen years, meets Donna Julia, aged twenty-three, at half past six. He felt entitled to an English summer day because the place was Canada.

[76]

FROST: Alyssum was blooming among the trees, yet he was disappointed.

FIRE: He was tired by the time he walked into the forest glade surviving for a few seasons high amidst the horizontal lights deflecting from icy plains and cliffs, too tired to see the idea of the image he was about to see by brushing watercolor words over low reliefs of feeling. He waited for some ogre or troll of truth.

FROST: While he waited, verses rubbed over the intaglio of feelings.
"I will not be untrue and take a wife.
I'll keep the holy vows I've made to Life."

FIRE: He looked up from the lichened rocks and the ferns, trying to remember facts about spores. A seed floated by toward ice.
"Forgive me, Althea, but I am wed to Life.
By laws of love and nature you could only be my second wife."

FROST: The honeysuckle did grow an improbable few feet from the ice, but it looked desultory, with lusterless leaves. He would have cracked open a stone to look for fossils, but he had no tools. The mosses differed among themselves obscurely. Some true feeling was escaping because he could not name it.

FIRE: Dreamy, drowsy, he loosened his collar and lay down upon the blanket he had carried. He thought of masturbating, and so to distract himself and to prepare himself he stood up and urinated onto the ice. He left his trousers unbuttoned.

FROST: He did not feel cold. The improbability of lying in

this unlikely forest intensified his dreamy happiness. Then he did feel the cold. The sun was setting. The surface of the glaciers seemed to contain its own light. "I will not take for wife
A woman less intense than Life."

FIRE: But what did he mean by Life that was different from Althea?

FROST: He ignored his hand in his trousers pulling his penis into a comfortable position. Perhaps the date, June sixth, was wrong. When did a new century begin? Perhaps in spring. He would count from March, like Chaucer, and then September would be the seventh month, and October, November, December would be eighth, ninth, and tenth. Where had he been in March? Next year he would celebrate with Althea. "I will not take for wife
A helpmeet less than Life."
The lines should be sinuous. Or more sinewy. He thought of Chaucer's springtime landscapes. Perhaps he was descended from Chaucer.

FIRE: An absent-minded hand rubs a nonchalant penis.

FROST: Estimating an average generation at 33⅓ years, three a century, as indeed his parents were in their early thirties when he was born in 1882. Hence two ancestors in 1866, four in 1833, eight in 1800, sixteen great-great grandparents in 1766.

FIRE: And half-dreaming numbers now, thinking of young married men and women, old women and men who had been young once.

FROST: And the numbers continued, 32 in 1733, young and

[78]

perhaps in love, 64 in 1700, 128 in 1666, 256 in
1633, 512 in 1600, passing Shakespeare now, and
Queen Elizabeth, 1,024 in 1566, his hand moving up
and down, and 2,048 in 1533, calculations growing
more difficult, one number growing larger, the other
smaller, 4,096 in 1500, losing focus, 8,192 in 1466,
feeling pressure increasing, each child represents one
orgasm, and 16,384 ancestors in 1433, so 8,192 men
in orgasm, 32,768 ancestors alive in 1400, approaching Chaucer, too diffused to multiply by two, dividing
by two again for the number of men gasping into
fatherhood on their women, 16,384, and 16,384 beds,
or beds of leaves and flowers, or haystacks, sheets and
blankets, against walls, skirts, codpieces, and then
his first cousin he had seen falling from the board-
walk onto the sand in her bathing costume and numbers dissolved as the semen burst into his handkerchief which he had methodically wrapped around
his penis and which he now carefully folded around
it even as his shoulders involuntarily struggled into
the air, and he fell back breathing *Althea* as above
his island of forest the lake water which had chilled
until it encroached upon the interior of ice lifted the
glacier, the surge of water rushing ahead of the
avalanches, picking him up, the handkerchief
clutched in the spasm of his fist, the couplet clarified
to crystal,
"I will not take for wife
A helpmate less than Life."
FIRE: As the onrush of water through the glade furled him

[79]

into its force and it spun into and back into a crevice, wrapping him in a crystal shoud which summer storms would vitrify with shards of ice until he was opaquely casketed in glacial intensity.

FROST: 1366: 65,536.
FIRE: 131,072.
FROST: 262,144 in 1300.
FIRE: 524,288.
FROST: 1,048,576 in 1233.
FIRE: 1200: 2,097, 152.
FROST: 4,194,304 in 1166.
FIRE: 8,388,608 in 1133.
FROST: 16,777,216.

III. 1982

TEXT: She calls herself Volterra.
CONTEXT: She has not earned the name.
TEXT: She uses it while she looks for the word that will give meaning to the sentence that gives meaning to the word.
CONTEXT: She does whatever she wants to.
TEXT: Not quite. She has pitched a tent on the ice where she performs experiments. Within the surface of the glaciers is a niche that some life finds an opportunity to live in.
CONTEXT: Why does she run naked on the ice?
TEXT: There she goes, not quite naked, woven slippers on her feet. The incidence of light upon the ice strikes her as an idea that she can't yet formulate. She

feels flashes of color breaking out of blue-white light.

CONTEXT: She does not catch the idea interwoven in the feeling of the ambient light, the radiant light, and her twirling naked on the field of ice.

TEXT: The experiment is a success so far. Her face and arms are still warm, her legs and stomach tingle with feeling. She breathes deeply and feels air in her throat.

CONTEXT: And the slippers.

TEXT: The slippers. She keeps her feet sensitive until she is ready to walk on bare feet across the ice without losing feeling in her feet. She can walk now, look, she walks now, naked across the glacial field, and feels the cold without losing the feeling of cold. She walks until she feels the loss of feeling, and when she knows that she has reached the boundary she runs into her tent aware of numbness.

CONTEXT: She is beautiful.

TEXT: Yes, an image of an improbable future desired but not despaired of. Between past and future and from left to right she is about to be but never is symmetrical.

CONTEXT: Does she know about the boy?

TEXT: She must seem to find him for herself. Look how she lies on the ice now, concentrating past the tingles splintering in her skin to feel vibrations in the glacial pack.

CONTEXT: She can feel more cold without less feeling now.

TEXT: She takes off her slippers and lies outstretched, her breasts against the ice.

CONTEXT: She runs, challenging shadows by walking under the overhanging cliffs of ice, and now into a crevice that opened in the night, feeling always the encroachment of unfeeling from the cold, but persisting in feeling the advances of unfeeling. . . .

TEXT: And now the shadow in the ice.

CONTEXT: His arms folded against his chest, his body diagonally lodged in ice. She puts her ear to the ice, and in a double auscultation hears the reverberations in the glacier and the echo of the bloodstream in her ear. She calculates the fissures in the ice.

TEXT: On the threshold of unfeeling, she feels a frisson when peering through the ice; then, too cold to be aware of cold, she runs to the tent. His grave will not break open in the night, her ear has told her. Wait until morning. Supper in the tent.

IV.

I woke at six and checked the experiments for thermotropism that I have deployed in the pattern of a quincunx down the glacis. Microorganisms living near the surface of the ice can move into the sterile nutritive medium that is kept at body temperature. I am looking for protozoa that can live usefully in a human host. Those that move from the ice to the body-warmth solution will have selected themselves. Ice is alive with fungus. Some of the microorganisms are from my body, but if they move through the ice into the solution they reveal a potentiality for surviving low temperatures or an ability to mutate rapidly in order to survive those temperatures, while retaining an attraction to warmth.

By six-thirty I stood in the fissure where I found him. The rays of the sun lay horizontally along a line from the horizon, and sunlight flashed and reflected in lines and splashes of light deep into the chamber. I had run there fully dressed, but now I quickly undressed, remembering to feel with my feet as I chipped the ice along the fractures. The sun rose, so exactly in a line with the crevice that it continued to illuminate my work. The first few crusty layers fell away. I put my ear to the ice, felt its grain, and chopped. Then he lay before me, pale in an unbuttoned leather jacket, a bandana in his hand, high shoes, trousers of some rough tweed, the first completed person I have seen, whose rescue for the future rescues me from the future I have been rehearsing. At last unrehearsed, I worked the bandana out of his fist and unfolded it as it softened to my touch. I took the billfold and a few papers from the pockets of the coat, and ran out of the crevasse carrying the handkerchief, my clothes, and a phallic shard of ice.

I lay on my back in the sunlight dispersing itself along the glacis until I was an experiment in diathermy. I wrapped the bandana inside out around the staff of ice, and inserted it, feeling the cold, then feeling the cold obscuring feeling, and I moved the rod slowly in and out, up and down, as it slowly melted, shaping itself to me as I shaped myself to it, and I contracted and let go, contracted and let go, gripping the rod as I shoved it deeper into myself, and letting go as it emerged, gripping and letting go, gripping and letting go,

[83]

and water warmed to the temperature of my body and overflowed onto my thighs, and I thought, Well, they'll swim for
it or they won't, and then my contractions overflowed themselves, my heart splintered asunder and then coalesced anew,
and I fell back upon my glacial bed, breathless to feel the
feeling of the ice within me, and nothing of me so numbed
that I could not feel numbness. When the shard of ice had
disappeared and warm water lay in puddles on my belly, I
stood up, climbed to the top of the crevice above the body,
and hit with the pick in a pattern that the complicit sunlight
would complete into an avalanche with the help of the next
cold dawn. I checked my experimental stations for microorganisms, the little traps I set for thermotropic somethings.

Note: The bandana tests for glycerol. Tonight I discovered
a luminescent fungus on my labia majora. I have transplanted half of it into a petri dish for cultivation, and left
the other half to grow.

V. 2000

VITO: I am so alone that I am embarrassed.
MIRROR: I didn't hear you.
VITO: I am a stand-in for incompleteness.
MIRROR: Leave the cave.
VITO: I can't. I am interested in nothing and afraid of
everything. They prosper here.
MIRROR: You could simulate these conditions elsewhere.
VITO: You don't understand me. I want to be left alone
to see myself. I have acquiesced in my own un-
acquaintance with anything but me.

[84]

MIRROR: You aren't seeing yourself, only the bioluminescent fungus and bacteria.

VITO: They cover me now in parti-colored colonies as far as I can see.

MIRROR: You see the phosphorescence of fungi which have sent their filaments into you. The parasites living on or within the fungi are living on what you produce.

VITO: They enable me to see myself in the darkness of this cave.

MIRROR: You see protozoa or metazoa, not yourself.

VITO: I have cultivated them on my body. When I was a child, I glowed in a few small patches here and there on my skin. I have developed new strains of luminescent fungi and these mutations that live on me are mine.

MIRROR: They feed on chemicals that you produce. The nitrogen whose electronic excitement luminesces as a long-lived yellow or short-lived pink afterglow. . . .

VITO: . . . is me, yes, yet as I am I am a man produced by the consumption of predacious luminescent fungi.

MIRROR: You could have been rich.

VITO: The plan to sue for my share of my father's estate. . . . My mother discovered from papers in his pocket. . . . His large fortune, inherited from paternal grandparents, enlarged by gifts. . . . Trust funds and holdings in real estate. . . . Paintings which he collected as birthday presents from his parents, 1890 to 1900 . . . which they inherited. . . . A black ormolu box, a grandfather's clock, an oxblood vase brought from China on a clipper ship. . . . "Your father would have wanted to provide for his son."

MIRROR: The case could have been made.

VITO: I chose to choose the events that chose me. The reconstructed parlor in the university museum furnished with his property, the portrait before which Volterra said I was the picture of my father, the implications from the furniture crossing and crisscrossing behind the red velvet guard-rope, the ethics of comfort. . . .

MIRROR: And the ethics of discomfort.

VITO: His foulard which took courage for him to wear. When Volterra gave up the use of reservoirs of body-temperature solutions to attract thermotropic microorganisms and used her eurythermal body, immersed in ice or in hot springs, the amoeba which moved into her body from the river water at Rio Caliente consumed her, those endoparasites which now in attenuated strains are used in laboratories to generate the growth of beneficial phagocytes.

MIRROR: Volterra was a laboratory. She experimented on you.

VITO: I bred the fungi myself. She taught me how to name the exoparasites, but I chose the fungus, spread the spores. Here on my forearm I cultivate a strain which glows with erythrismal light.

MIRROR: Your ankles and wrists are glowing, and your neck.

VITO: Yes, I can see.

MIRROR: Now the light is dimming.

VITO: Yes, as I notice the light, it diminishes.

MIRROR: Your face is bright.

VITO: I said that I am embarrassed. When I think about the luminescence, it fades.

MIRROR: Your back hasn't changed.

VITO: I don't want to know.

MIRROR: There where you touch your shoulder, a green fluorescence.

VITO: Biotriboluminescence. It doesn't mean anything.

MIRROR: A frostbitten light exudes along your spine.

VITO: A fungal phosphorescence.

MIRROR: Beautiful.

VITO: Let me see.

MIRROR: The light subsides along your backbone as correlative of your awareness.

VITO: I will forget to think about it.

MIRROR: The bacteria and fungus call attention to themselves. See the glow. You can read it for yourself.

VITO: I am the only one who can look at it. I must see it.

MIRROR: Now the luminescence dims. Look at your back.

VITO: Where are you? Don't disappear now.

MIRROR: I haven't disappeared. As you think about the light on your back it fades.

VITO: I cannot not think about it. But I can't see you anymore.

MIRROR: You are looking at me. It's yourself you cannot see.

ANTHROPOLOGY: WHAT IS LOST IN ROTATION

... we take it that:
mouth : ear : : vagina : anus

—Lévi-Strauss,
The Raw and the Cooked

bouche : oreille : : vagin : anus

—*Le Cru et le Cuit*

I.

That you want to give me pleasure gives me as much pleasure as what you do to give me pleasure.

Translation: you don't feel satisfied.

No, I don't.

Don't tell me what you think I want to hear.

I am pleased by your desire to please me.

But you are unsatisfied.

Yes, I am.

Now you have told me the truth, and I realize that I prefer the truth, at least the truth I would have suspected anyway, to what I think I want to hear, and I am proud of myself again, and forgive you as I respect myself, and now I love you again. But you are still unsatisfied.

You weren't thinking about me when you were inside me. You were trying to distract me so that you could be alone. So don't complain that I wasn't with you.

When I married an Englishwoman studying English literature at the Sorbonne I underestimated the difficulties. Don't underestimate yourself. Actually I was thinking about an Indian boy I want to arrest for murder.

[88]

Yes, you made love to me as though you were looking for a clue.

I think the accused is entitled to one quotation: "Men owe us what we imagine they will give us. We must forgive them this debt." Simone Weil.

I have a quotation too. "I also am other than what I imagine myself to be. To know this is forgiveness." *"Moi aussi, je suis autre que ce que je m'imagine être. Le savoir, c'est le pardon."*

II.

But then you can't arrest him, you have no evidence.

The evidence is that four structural anthropologists have died, apparently poisoned, and each of them had done field work in his village.

But you say they worked there a decade ago, when he was a child. Where is the motive?

The motive is mine. I can't leave the mystery of four similar simultaneous deaths.

Why do you think the murderer is this Indian?

Why do you think this Indian lives in Paris?

He has told you. He worked his way to Paris translating for anthropologists and missionaries in an attempt to discover his father, the anthropologist who left him with nothing but the name Emile. You need a criminal, and out of that need you have constructed Emile.

I have many needs besides the need for a criminal. These four victims were once a model team of anthropologists, two husbands and two wives, able to study both the men and women intimately. A great loss to the Sorbonne. Emile intends to study their book for patterns to use when he returns to rebuild his society.

Where is he going to study anthropology, in prison?

No, Emile is not going to prison. We don't have enough evidence to hold him. He wants to find out who named him, that is, who his father was, and he wants to learn enough about his people to restore them to the rightness he thinks he remembers from his childhood. He may also solve the mystery of the murders.

You are letting him go free so that he can convict himself? The procedure sounds too literary to be legal.

He has chosen to play detective himself, searching for an anthropologist who left him a name, whether sardonically or tenderly, who knows? And why does he search for him? To understand himself? To kill his father? I don't know. I am too old to learn anthropology, yet someone has to find clues to the murders. Emile has come to Paris looking for the secret of himself. If he finds the murderer for us, and the murderer is himself, then we may be able to help him.

If he committed the murders, why doesn't he confess?

You have touched upon the mystery. Emile is capable of killing, but I'm not sure he can be the murderer because so far he is incapable of understanding murder. The clue I look for in a homicide is the clue that tells me which suspect is capable of murder.

Yes, since I can hide nothing from you, I do almost nothing that I would have to hide from you except the doing of nothing that I would have to hide from you. I would not be able to conceal from you that I had killed a man, but I would try to conceal from you that I am capable of killing.

Perhaps you will help Emile to understand.

Me? What would I say to him?

He will be living in our apartment. The condition under which he can remain in Paris and attend the Sorbonne is that he be French. The government cannot hold him indefinitely without charges. You and I are adopting him as our son.

I wonder how he can trust you since you think he killed four people. Suppose he kills you?

I don't see that he would have a motive. He is not a savage.

I don't know. I don't think that anyone outside Paris can understand love and murder as we do.

But Emile loves Paris, and loving Paris is a murderous education.

III.

Inspector Mirouet?

Yes, Emile?

I am writing a paper on anderology. Perhaps you would correct the grammar?

I don't know the word, Emile. *Anthropology*, perhaps?

No, Inspector. The question is the origins of cooking over a fire.

I thought that Lévi-Strauss had solved that forty years ago.

Yes, of course, but I have some new materials coded for the computer. I am afraid that they will not seem polite.

They will weather that shock at the Sorbonne, Emile.

I understand that, Inspector. But my paper will seem rude to the English, perhaps.

Then we will not show it to the English, Emile, unless you

want my wife's help with it. Perhaps you should tell me first.

The word for a hot coal carried to a fireplace to start a fire is *bitch*.

The English will take that in stride, Emile.

And the bitch is carried to the firedogs, just as the female is carried to the male dog to be lined. The French for firedog is *andier*, from the Gaulish *andero*, young bull. The origins of fire are shown in the image of carrying a bitch to a dog for breeding. The female comes to the male to start a fire. The male goes to the female to put out a fire. I will explain the story of Europa and the bull, and the scene on the Vaphio gold cup. Are you laughing at me, Inspector?

No, Emile. I am merely recalling how Madame Mirouet and I met.

Is it polite for me to ask how you met, Inspector?

Of course, Emile. Haven't I told you? I was a student of anderology doing field work at the Sorbonne.

IV.

Inspector Mirouet?

Yes, Emile?

I have found a curious gap in Professor Lévi-Strauss' information.

You know something that he didn't know?

I doubt that. But he professes not to know the meaning of the word *reyuno*. I have found the word in my memory, and also in the computer data bank. It is a rude word for penis.

I never heard the word, Emile. Perhaps Lévi-Strauss simply didn't know it.

I won't believe that, Inspector. Anyone who worked along the coast would have learned that meaning. The apparent ignorance of the word must be an example of upward displacement of ignorance. Not to understand the word, which seems to me impossible, is not to understand the thing, which is possible. When this upward displacement is redisplaced downwards, and then upwards again, something will be out of line, but the system will seek to preserve its coherence even if it loses correspondence with the facts.

Where did you learn to think like this, Emile?

At the Sorbonne, Inspector, reading Lévi-Strauss.

V.

Inspector?

Yes, Emile?

I want to return to Brazil now.

That isn't possible, Emile. We aren't ready. Has anything frightened you?

I am going to hide it from you, Inspector.

What is it, Emile. Has someone hurt you?

I have hurt myself, Inspector. I will never be able to restore my people to their beautiful ways. I have found an upward displacement in the system of structural anthropology which I was going to use to rebuild my society with simplicity and symmetry, and the whole system is distorted by an error in rotation. I can use none of it.

Explain it, Emile. Perhaps it isn't as bad as you think.

I will be patient, but this spoils everything. Damn Rousseau.

What does Rousseau have to do with it, Emile? I can't keep up with you.

You know that Rousseau suffered from enuresis and hypospadias.

Enuresis I know, but what is hypospadias?

A deformity of the penis. The urethra opens on its under surface. I am afraid that after Rousseau's hypospadias subsequent upward displacements in French thought are rotated incorrectly.

This is a strong charge, Emile. Are you sure of the evidence?

I am afraid that I am.

Do not be reluctant to expose error, Emile. We will be pleased to learn our mistakes.

But I am not pleased to tell you. My people, my family, are scattered in hospitals and reservations, and I was going to reunite them.

You may yet, Emile. Perhaps the mistake can be corrected.

You are patriotic, Inspector, but this logical scandal is not easily mitigated. Lévi-Strauss knew it, too. In *From Honey to Ashes* he asks, "Which organ, then, can be defined as posterior and high in a system in which the posterior, low position is occupied by the anus, and the anterior, high position by the mouth? We save no choice: it can only be the ear. . . ." He goes on to write that ". . . vomiting is the opposite correlative of coitus, and defecation the opposite correlative of auditory communications," but the ear is not in front, like the vagina, or behind, like the anus. My grandmother held me by the ears, or pulled my nose; sometimes she patted me on the crown of my head. We know the back of the head from an ear. The rest of mythologic is distorted by the translation of Rousseau's urethra, and I am afraid that I can be of no help here, and of no help to my people. But at least I know what I must do next.

What are you going to do?

With your permission, Inspector, have my occipital bone X-rayed and enroll in medical school.

VI.

Inspector?

Yes, Emile?

Let me read these X-rays with you. Notice this dark spot on the occipital. Here it is, from the left. And here, from the right. Do you see it?

Just a shadow, Emile. I can't tell if there is something there or something missing.

A scar, Inspector. Here, you can feel it on my head when you know where it is.

Yes, I feel something. What can you figure out from the scar, Emile?

The four anthropologists could not determine what occurred in the huts to which women retired for childbirth, where a mother and child stayed for a few weeks. The myths require a hole in the occipital region. When a male baby was born, the mother trephined a hole in the back of the head and removed some brain tissue.

How can you know this from Paris, Emile?

Because that is where the coroner's reports are. You think

that I hid behind potted palms and blew poisoned darts at four professors. But the clues you needed to their deaths were there at the Sorbonne, in their behavior.

I did not see them, and the doctors did not recognize the symptoms of a disease.

They trembled, they swayed and spun around as though they were doing a parody of a native dance, they became stiff, threw fits, and then went into comas and died.

Did any of your people die that way?

I trust my memory that the most powerful man in the village would start having seizures, and would think himself possessed by that spirit we named "the weather of elsewhere." Then he would die, and life would continue like a story about life until another man became boastful, and he would sicken and die. This happened so slowly that I don't know if it broke the rhythm of our lives or gave our lives their rhythm.

Have you figured out the cause?

I can only speculate. The highlanders of New Guinea were cannibals and suffered deaths similar to those of the anthropologists. The disease is called *kuru*, and is caused by a slow-acting virus. Research has been slow, for animals infected with the virus can take three or four years before they show any symptoms.

Your people are not cannibals, however.

No, but I have had the skulls of children from my tribe examined, and have received reports from laboratories and museums that have skulls of Indians. Lévi-Strauss was right. Logic requires an orifice high and posterior, and since one was not there, the mother, hidden in the hut after the birth of the baby, drilled a small hole in the back of the baby's head.

For God's sake why?

They could not know. I suppose they had to complete a pattern: ".... *les mythes se pensent dans les hommes, et à leur insu.*" They would extract some brain tissue, mix it in a dish, and serve it to certain men.

To kill them?

No, the women could not make that connection. After all, although the disease acts swiftly once it reveals itself, it can take years to develop.

Do you know how your people caught the disease?

I don't know that it is a disease. A virus that is benign is transferred from brain to brain and deteriorates into molecules of RNA without protein coats, or into naked strands of DNA. The virus may be innocent, but something can happen to it when it enters the host cell. The host cell seems to transform a virus into a viroid, and years later death ensues. So your four anthropologists. . . .

Yes, Emile?

Your four anthropologists wanted to participate in the lives of my people in order to understand them. They might have told the men of my tribe that they were longing to taste some dish, and neither the men nor the anthropologists could have known that the women had mixed in the brains of children.

Why did no one figure this out?

The anthropologists were studying my people synchronically. They missed the narrative of disease, although they brought it with them here to Paris, where they created a mystery about my people and about me.

You seem to have solved the mystery, Emile.

I don't know, Inspector. When I return to Brazil I will do research. I think that there may be a transmissible canine encephalopathy, one that slowly destroys the cerebellum and the hypothalamus.

You are formidable, Emile. I accuse you of murder, and you solve a mystery and construct hypotheses about disease that might save other lives. Are you bitter, Emile? Do you seek revenge?

No, no revenge. My people are murdered, hospitalized or thrown together on reservations. I would like to find them and kindle a family of families that would compose itself like a flame. I don't know the possibilities. But I remember a place that I will take them to where the water falls from a cliff into a pool. In the cave under the waterfall we will kindle a fire. And I will explain to them that our lives should, as the water and flame do, find their own patterns.

An ambitious program, Emile, inventing a society.

I don't intend to invent it. I mean only to be the improbable accident that starts the fire that continues to burn according to the probabilities of fire. I want to found a village in the forest. The nights are long under the waterfall around the fire, just as they are in Paris. I will tell stories of my journey to Paris, and I will tell them about Jean-Jacques Rousseau and the night a girl with a withered nipple tried to seduce him.

You hate us more than we hate ourselves, Emile.

No, Inspector. I was reading that story when I paused to

think about asymmetry, and while scratching the back of my head, I felt the little scar that gave me an idea.

And your father, Emile? You came to Paris to find out who named you. The anthropologist who probably was your father. Have you found him?

No, Inspector. The stories of young men searching for their fathers are stories of young men who through their adventures father themselves by doing for themselves what they hoped a father would do for them. You adopted me, half-Indian, half-comprador, after you found me parading up and down waiting for someone to read me as a clue. I was not looking for my father. He died of a slow-acting virus, if I remember his death correctly. I named myself Emile. What would I need a father for?

VII.

Emile.

Yes, Madame.

What are you reading?

A book about Brazil. The unexplored parts are photographed by satellites. I am thinking about a place where my people will be safe.

I am married to an Inspector of Police in Paris, Emile, and I don't feel safe.

The case is somewhat different. Where is the Inspector tonight, Madame?

He has been called to Marseilles, Emile. I don't know why. He'll return tomorrow.

And what are you reading, Madame?

Actually I was looking for two passages I had thought to

read aloud to you. They remind me of your descriptions of
the life you hope to start in Brazil. Let me take off these
earrings and then I'll read them to you.

Why do you remove your earrings?

Haven't you heard the Inspector say to me, "A French-
woman, after she has finished dressing, always removes one
piece of jewelry."

But you are not French, Madame.

A point I invariably make to him, Emile. Let me read you
the passages, and then I want you to tell me about the cave,
the waterfall, and the fire.

I am ready to listen, Madame.

Coleridge wrote, "Most of my readers will have observed
a small water-insect on the surface of rivulets, which throws
a cinque-spotted shadow fringed with prismatic colours on
the sunny bottom of the brook; and will have noticed, how
the little animal *wins* its way up against the stream, by
alternate pulses of active and passive motion, now resisting
the current, and now yielding to it in order to gather strength
and a momentary *fulcrum* for a further propulsion. This is
no unapt emblem of the mind's self-experience in the act of
thinking."

I think, Madame, that you would make a creditable Indian.

I haven't found it easy being an Englishwoman in Paris,
Emile.

Yet Paris is a seductive city.

Then you understand me, Emile?

Yes, Madame.

I have another passage to read to you first. It describes you.
Coleridge wrote of a tree, "At the same moment it strikes its

roots and unfolds its leaves, absorbs and respires, steams forth its cooling vapor and finer fragrance, and breathes a repairing spirit, at once the food and tone of the atmosphere, into the atmosphere that feeds it."

I can't understand English when it is read aloud to me, Madame, but I will take the water-insect as my totem, and tell my people a story about an imaginative woman who seduces an Indian boy with metaphors.

VIII.

Emile?

Don't turn around.

I want to hold you. With you I don't feel sensations, I feel you.

Look out the window at the lime tree. Have you decided who I am?

No, I don't recognize you, yet I know what you are. You are immediacy.

Don't turn around. Look out the window and tell me what you see.

I see a lime tree in the first light of a Parisian dawn. I see Paris filled to the brim.

Don't look back.

Your hands don't hesitate.

I don't look behind us.

Your hands on my hips. I know who you are now and why I'm not afraid. You aren't afraid of yourself.

Don't turn around. I am looking past your head at what you see through the window. I can feel that you enjoy my hands.

I do. I like your fingers across my hips and your kisses on my back.

Don't turn around.

I want to see you but I can wait. I want to feel your hands there, yes, like that. I was going to forgive you for not giving me this pleasure that I had imagined for myself. I no longer need to. I have become as immediate to myself as you are to me, yet now your immediacy equals your indeterminacy. Let me turn around to see you.

No, I want to stand behind you, touching you with my fingers.

Do what I asked you to, Emile.

Only if you forgive yourself for imagining that you could live there.

I forgive myself when your flesh touches mine. You know what I want to hear.

You should ask.

I want to hear about the waterfalls and the streams and the trees, and the families you will gather to lead into the jungle. I want you to describe the splash of the falls, the deep cave, the flames that are kindled and that flicker and waver and renew their shape, and the skills you use, without bridges or boats, to help each other across impassable streams.

. . . And not enough food, twenty exhausted people, crying children, cold, damp.

Then what is it, Emile? I am not sentimental, I wear expensive but sensible shoes, and I am not going to become an Indian.

What do you feel now?

Strange. The feeling is so vivid, yet it disappears when I reach for it with words.

Don't reach. Let it surround you. Then you have it, when it has you. Stand up to it.

You can leave now, Emile. I know enough not to turn around.

Are you satisfied with that?

Yes, strangely, I am. I wonder why you have done this for me.

That is the question I will leave you with, and then I'll never have left you, and that will be to perform yet another act that must make you wonder why I have done it, and thus you will always feel me behind you, one hand over your *bouche*, like this, with a finger on your teeth, and the other hand over your *vagin*, like this, and me whispering into your hair *une pensée de derrière*, that I could crush your skull against the window frame.

INTERIM

For that half-hour in the hospital delivery room I was intimate with immensity, for that half-minute before birth I held her hands and for that duration we three were undivided, I felt the blood of her pulse as we gripped hands, felt her blood beat in the rhythm that reached into the baby as she slipped into the doctor's hands, and for a few days we touched that immensity, we saw through her eyes to an immense intimacy, saw through to where she had come from, I felt important being next to her, and the feeling lasted when we entered our car for the drive home, thinking to myself that we weren't to be trusted with our baby, the feeling lasting while I measured us against the landscape, the February rain, the pewter sky, and then the rain freezing to the roadway, the warmth of the interior of the car with its unbreakable transparent skydome and doors, until the car spun on the ice in the lane and twirled so that I could take an hour to describe how I threw up my hands in anguish as the baby slipped from her arms and whipped into the face of her mother reflected in the glass door, and she caught the baby back into her arms as the car glided to a stop in its usual place at the end of the drive, and nothing but silence and a few drops of blood at a nostril suggested that we would now be intimate with the immensities of death.

I tried to say to the man that I wanted her buried in a canvas bag, to return to earth the sooner, but he declined to hear anything I said until I said what was appropriate for him to hear, which I thought was an agreement that she should be buried in a pine box, without embalming or other sophistications—I would myself and I did right then weave orange ribbons into the dress to take the sting out of so much pink—but the bill when it came said "lead-lined" so that her body I continue to think will be badly preserved forever, but then I have no way to know what happened, for the under-taker is dead in the forest now, and the ground was still frozen then, he would not have been able to bury her until later in the spring when I was on my way and so did not go to my daughter's funeral at the back of the graveyard. Later I planted a circle of larches in the middle of a moor, and years after that, even though Scotch pines had grown around it and within it, I traced the circle of trees, an unending rap-port of larches.

When I arrived home from the hospital for the second time that day, without the baby, driving fast, the sky was black. No lights in the house. I walked upstairs in the dark, but my feet remembered every footstep toward the bed. I lay down heavily and sighed. "She is dead, isn't she," Rosabianca asked. "Yes," I answered, "of course," and I suppose we knew the way we turned toward each other and with each other that every hesitation and grievance and regret were meeting every reluctance and reservation and doubt in unrepentant fare-well, we yielded to each other in mutual chagrin without a

[105]

thought or a kiss, and when an aloof light shone through the window, an excuse to call it morning, I sat up, and saw on my pillowcase the legible and indelible red print of my hand which had inked itself with blood from between her thighs, not enough for her to die from, I supposed, and I suffixed the words I had to say with a hiss I hoped she would not hear, "murderess of breaths," and I left, taking only what I had earned, a look, the tearful version of the first dry look I caught and then forgot, the look that stayed throughout our marriage behind the smile, the look that now inherited her face, an anticipation of grief that tempted me to try to make her happy, her foreknowledge of the tyrannies of sorrow, somber reds underlying golds, the bitterness that inspired her to call me "Butterscotch," I helpless against the terrorism in her love, the pathos of a woman's flesh touched by shadows, this woman I had found in the hills beyond Trieste, to whom I taught English with a few Scotticisms as she taught me resistance, I explaining that *kilt* was correct, not *kilts*, and that yes, some people now used *kilts* for a woman's skirt that looked like a kilt, but that she would never, when she came from Jugoslavia to be my Scottish bride, never wear a tartan or a plaid. She shrugged agreement to everything except my plea not to be called "Butterscotch," because my hair, my beard, hairs on my fingers and along my wrists, my eyebrows, whatever sun touched was indeed butterscotch, and I knew I was so dour that I should accept the playfulness, although the lovename never sounded right to me any more than her Adriatic beauty looked at home in our Scottish light or worse, on skimpy days, our Scottish lack of light.

That week I trudged across Scotland. I walked accompan-

ied by rushing salmon streams or gently flowing rivers, fol-
lowed by children and dogs, and I walked beyond towns,
across barren heaths, through marshes, and in the falling
rain I walked down a long hill following a stream that led
to a cottage where I took tea and scones. I stood on hillsides
gazing at the total sky, and one evening I sat leaning against
the stone wall on the light side, and watched the sunset as
my idea of the baby caught in amber light above the firth,
and I climbed over to the night side of the wall and crouched
with the darkness leaning toward me, and then I slept. In
the morning I began the north-east walk back to our house.

Rosabianca was gone. She was gone, the baby was in the
refrigerator at the hospital, the car stood in the lane. I opened
the bubble-door at the back and saw growing on the carpet
a gray-green plant. Sometimes I feel that the last believable
moment of my life that I remember was smiling at Rosabianca across the top of the car as we got in to drive to the
hospital, and sometimes, because the accident seems so unnecessary, the first convincing memory is the glimpse of that
plant.

I drove south toward the coast, where spring comes sooner,
and in a plant nursery bought the larches, and threw them
into the back of the car with some flats of various plants to
see, as I more or less lived in the car, which seedlings would
thrive in my mobile greenhouse. I learned to move the car
according to the time of day, to park it for the most advan-
tageous light. I would drive and park in a town, and once,
returning to the car, surprised to find a crowd standing
around it, I waited my turn to see what they were seeing,
and then, looking into my car with the eyes of thrifty strang-

ers, I conceived my plan for the reforestation of Scotland.

I don't believe that the Scots were always frugal, now that I have read our mean history. Once the land was without mankind and was covered with trees—most of these heaths and moors are modern—and heather grows on the moor because the peasants snapped the limbs they could reach from the trees as high as they could reach, which slowed the growth of the trees, and their pigs rooted up saplings in the forest, and with branches beyond reach men chopped down the trees, trees that had leeched the shallow soil but at least held it with their roots, so that with fewer trees the rains carried off the thin layer of soil, trees became more scarce, winds blew wilder, dry land grew drier and wet land grew more wet, as one peasant here and another peasant there, gathering infinitesimal sticks for paltry winter fires, first raised the trees into the shapes of trees in a medieval hunting scene, and a courtier or if you will a laird might ride horseback through the forest, which looked as cultivated as he did, and he might hunt stags or roes visible among the visible trunks of allegorical trees, as allegory to us was naturalism to them, but their trim and vertical forests quickly deforested to vacant heath and moor, sheep and cattle grazing, nothing much taller than heather, and stone cottages built, a small dairy, smoke curling from chimneys in the morning, thick blue-grey ascending into blue, the old landshape become a landscape, and stones shaped into walls that curved with hilly fields, poisonously quaint, so that modern Scotland—Scotland by the seventeenth century—has been gardened, with no un-policied nature anywhere, and the only worse yet to come the townscape, the rustic villages, towns shaped with a view

to the view, town hall spire rhyming with church steeple, a
skyline constructed because they saw themselves as others
would see them as they drove around the curve of the road,
and they wanted to be ready for them, one tree left at the
margin of a hill to catch the sunset in its branches, a grove
of trees in the middle of a city as a park or square or green,
the whole of Scotland a manshape, and the interferences of
men applauded everywhere by men as they drove out to
view the scenery and viewed the sum of infinitesimal greeds,
the history of Scottish appetites, uncalculated and incalulable
intrusions into the forest until the forest became a moor, and
as they stood chattering round my car, I saw my plan which
would cost me, as frugal as the next Scotsman, almost nothing, since I would use their frugality, for they appreciated
the thrift of my mobile greenhouse, the chance to start seedlings earlier in the year, and I economically gave away the
flats to those people, and thriftily bought more, and drove to
more and more townsquares, and quietly proselytized, and
I thought, well, let each one teach one, they'll learn if it will
seem to save a penny, and then easy it was, so easy, to begin
reforestation, for the mobiledome cars throughout Scotland
were soon thousands of greenhouses, and the rational plans
presented in newspapers and on television solved the problem the people were beginning to sense that they shared, as
they had more seedlings than they knew what to do with,
more seedlings than good sense, as some said, and they began
to plant them at the edge of the moors, and they drove out
on holiday and planted with an eye to the view, and threw
compost around, but the next crowd the following week had
its eye on yet another view, and so with cheerful anarchy they

cooperated with no one but they unwittingly cooperated with me as they replanted Scotland, and the greener it became, the more itself it looked, replanted not in one year, but within ten years, twenty years, until it was green, green, down into swamps, up against crags, and in thirty years downtown Glasgow too, and green to the very doors of cottages. The infinitesimal seedlings became a forest of trees that grew courteously, correcting the distances between themselves as they shaped themselves to the promptings of available light and moisture, tempering the climate and the temperaments of the Scots, as the driest land became moist and the wettest land became dry, seedlings finding a mean between extremes, and the trees constructing a moderate zone for themselves even into what I would have called tundra, until I understood the fact that Aristotle taught, while walking in a botanic garden, that the middle is fittest to discern the extremes.

Several years should now be measured in the rings of trees, in a dendrochronology, not in mere days. The weatherbeaten landscape shaped and reshaped itself to metal, earth, wind, fire, and water. For a few years people still built houses in the country, or drove out to view scenery, but gradually the moral of the landscape reached into them. They had only to look at the forests, to see the return of emblematic and heraldic animals, and they realized that man was unwelcome, and I think that the first emigration began before I circulated my plans, for while the emigration would not solve the problem, the emigrants were useful, apparent traitors to a national cause, and the same nationalism achieved the separation from England in order to pursue our national destiny, the Stone of Scone restored to Edinburgh, and destiny defined itself as the purification of Scotland, the elimination not alone of the English but of mankind from the landscape against which his poisonousness grew more apparent and more unbearable, and the movement seemed voluntary, in fact was voluntary in that I merely presented ideas from behind the scenes, and some people feeling the unwelcome sailed off sentimentally to Ireland in boats, as though the year were 1912, not 2012, cowards who thereby delineated the contours of noble action, so that while the idea was mine, the people knew without being told the correct act to perform, and throughout Scotland first a few men and women, many students, sometimes a vacationist who backpacked in the new wilderness, others in family groups, undressing and making piles of their earth-colored clothing—umber, ochre, and viridian—where they might be useful to a tree, lay down naked in a place that varied according to sensibility, perhaps romantically on the crest of a hill, or usefully in an erosion gulley, and again with a variety of means, because the suggestion was mine, but the act was theirs, idealists or pragmatists, perhaps opened their veins with a knife and let the blood flow into the soil, or drank a chemical that would be lethal to them but harmless to carrion or to the soil, and they, I think cheerfully and with relief, lay down and sacrificed themselves for the common good of Scotland, and certainly they looked satisfied to me, as I continued my long patrol, when I would come upon a body and feel as I felt when I recognized a word I had been looking for, a body lying in a spot that had been chosen to help a struggling tree, birds picking at the remaining flesh, veiled by webs of mold, insects marching along paths that circulated through the bones, parents and young children grouped together, having chosen to die together, and with pets—a dog that would have been helpless, a cat that would have killed too much other game, once a horse with its saddle mildewed in the grass beside it— and Scotland now shameless and pure, even the obstacles of stone houses yielding to seeds that rooted within cracks in the walls, and vines growing through windows left open for them. I continued my rounds, occasionally seeing one of the last few families arranging itself, and I would greet them and continue on my way, and gradually I overcame my fear of stumbling over a dead body in the forest, and I learned to nod in silent tribute. I thought of throwing lime onto the bodies, and then I thought, who am I to dance with wind and rain and animals, with frost and thaw and sunshine, and then for a year I neither saw nor heard a living person in Scotland, and my work was finished, at last I was feral and would find a place to die, but first I wanted to look across a vale from the height of a stony crag, and at my perch, leaning against the stone warmed by the sun, I ate my pemmican and then I slept, and when I woke I thought, yes, we have done decently, and even if that place was, because of its height, too dramatic, yet I resolved to die there as food for birds. Then I saw, down in the glen, elided syllables of smoke ascending from a cottage chimney into the inarticulate blue sky.

I admit that defiance excited me. Everyone had been so compliant, the reasonableness of the plan was so apparent, I had not had the chance to argue. I stood up, and walking carefully, not to break a branch that would soon break by itself, not to rearrange leaves that would serve a purpose as they were, not to frighten a single bird fetching a twig for its nest, I walked, the last or next to the last thing in Scotland that would be aware of itself or ashamed of itself, careful where I put my foot among the rhythms that I did not want to hasten or retard, and while my goal had been my death at the edge of the sublime, I would be satisfied if I reached that cottage in the vale.

I reached the cottage, but only as evening had settled into the valley, dusk arriving earlier among the dark trees than back on the crag that I had left. I walked through the thick growth of trees easily, for this was quite far north, and lower branches died and fell off from lack of sunlight, or deer browsed as high as they could reach, my innocent gardeners. When I reached the cottage, I had the feeling that I was keeping an appointment that I had not made, for there it held its ground, as primitive as it was primordial, and when I walked to a window and looked into the glass as into a mirror, I saw not so much myself as my idea of a hermit, white hair and beard, copper eyebrows. Walking around the cottage, which seemed, in its ungainly Scottish way, perfectly square, in order to have the minimum rectilinear exterior wall, I came to another window, and focusing beyond the glass, within the room, I saw a woman I recognized as my mother, although my mother, dead in the forest now, had not lived to be as old as that woman, and then the face turned and yielded its look to the window, and I recognized Rosabianca, so I had married a woman like my mother after all, or at least I had married into the matrix, although my mother had been opposed to me bringing a Slavic bride to Scotland,

and for a moment she peered close to the window, and my reflection for that moment was superimposed upon her face, and I knew that she heard footsteps but was unafraid, in fact that she was listening at the window, not looking through it, and then she stood straight and she was like no idea that I had ever had, and if once I had been in love, I knew that we were still within love, and ever the beauty of a woman who has not thought herself beautiful, and I heard her call "Allen" from the doorway, and walked around to where she stood drying her hands on a white apron.

I have heard about you, Allen. I sit by my fireside and think that you are dead.

I wanted to see my plan accomplished. The trees will seed the rest of the land. You are the only *partižanka* I have found.

I don't need to lie down in the forest and swallow seeds that would kill me and then grow out of my flesh. I can fall paralyzed to die on this hearth and be as much use here as anywhere. Worms will find me out, and the fly of that moment will be satisfied with my flesh in which to lay its eggs, or some vine reaching with a tendril for support will clasp my bone at just the right moment for that vine in that season. At last I can do nothing but what is useful, thanks to you. You are good enough for both of us, Allen.

Enough, Rosabianca, I never said that I was good, only that I felt guilty about spoiling or interfering. I wanted an unsophisticated Scotland.

Yes, Allen, you spoiled something that would have been perfect otherwise. Your stroll through the glade disrupted some order between the birds and the trees, and perhaps the world would have been better off without you. Now you are proud of this bad conscience of yours, Allen, and no one is alive to accuse you except your wife, your witness.

Why don't you sit down? You are still too beautiful to admit being uncomfortable.

I am not disarmed. In my country we knew about presumption. Yes. I like this vacated Scotland myself, but Scotland was not made to please me. You have filled it with moldering corpses while I sit thinking of the infant.

Infinite.

What did you say?

Nothing.

You are still rude. Yet something between us, I admit it.

I know what is between us. Between is between us, and between this between and the other between, an infinity of betweens, and I have never been any more or any less near to you than I am now, and these betweens futilely deny an obscure and infinite oblivion.

I am oblivious of infinity.

Because you love me. Without me, you feel the pain of ruptured infinities.

You are a twist in the universe, Allen, by which it curls back to see its assumptions, which it does see through you even as you see that you do not fit those assumptions, and so you recoil from yourself. How a universe would explain its vogue for you I can't imagine. Good night, Allen. My mother said that a wedding is a death, a death is a wedding. You can figure out some comfortable arrangement for yourself with these pillows if you can sleep.

Rosabianca sleeps as I write this memoir for her. As I write

[115]

it for you, Rosabianca, with whom I exchanged dialects. Scotland is mine again, and is green. When light breaks, I will walk into the forest of exquisitely differentiated greens —goodbye, Rosabianca—leaving you as my translation of its green language (leaving you as my translation of its green language into truth) (my translation of the green language of trees) (knowing that the green language of this forest is true if you are its translation) (true if it is translated into you) (the green language of this forest speaks the truth if it is translatable into you) (the green language true if you would but translate it) (transpose) (if you are its translation) (the green language true if you would but transpose it) (you and this green language translate one truth).

I did not sleep. I have read this sermon written by Allen. Of course I said almost none of this. Husbands and wives rarely call each other by their given names. Allen wished that I spoke like that so that I would sound like him. He was always fictional. "By fictional I mean twisted to fit an assumption." I was born among antiquities in the hills beyond Trieste during a truce, and I am an unlikely ingredient in the reforestation of Scotland. Awareness of continuity is the first discontinuity, and is tragic enough. Allen expects to make a difference by being translated into trees, as if to be were to be translatable. Let him rest comfortably upon his throne of skulls.

CONVEYANCE:
"THE STORY I WOULD NOT
WANT BILL WILSON TO READ."

Río Caliente

Dear Bill,

I was going to say that this letter is difficult to write, but then you would wonder why I am writing it, so I will not make it easy for me by saying that it is difficult, but simply go ahead, if I can. Even as I write to you now, I sense you not only as the reader of this letter, I sense you eavesdropping on me as I write it. I know that you are weary of being told that you intimidate the very people whom you encourage, and I know that you can tell yourself that whatever you did for me in commenting on my writing was for my good, but I felt caught in some circularity in which you could do no wrong, even your mistaken comments could be useful, if only as obstacles that would strengthen me if I could overcome them, as I tried to explain to you what I had meant, but I can't help thinking that you were often too interested in staking out some position for yourself beyond criticism or retaliation, that you have often been more interested in the rightness of your position than in helping me, admitting that I asked for the help but that you undertook to read what I wrote and to comment on it for purposes of your own which

[117]

CONVEYANCE

I have not questioned but which must have served some self-interest on your part. I am trying not to seem shrill for several reasons which I will spell out. Or perhaps I simply don't want to be shrill. Anyway you know how scattered my education was, but you don't know that I was never trained in being criticized, I had not learned to stop pretending ignorance or incompetence. A comment such as *ramshackle* on my story was new to me, and I think you underestimated the handicap of my education, its blandness, and while you remained bitter and spoke of the acid bath of criticism or of how you were patronized, you were being patronized in some of the best places while I was being educated to count linen in the suburbs, and you are tougher than you credit yourself with being (which encourages me to write this letter), and I was more hurt by your helpful suggestions—if only because I needed so much help—than I ever told you. Which is not to say that I also may not have misunderstood your comments.

Your last note to me was now almost two years ago. I've reread it, and I see both that you were covering yourself, wanting to be impressive in ways that seem to me contrary to the ways in which I do find you impressive—and so much of your ambition (which you did not admit to) is revenge (which you would not admit to)—and also that I misunderstood your final *assignment* or suggestion to me. You had given me, not the motifs for the stories, but the impulse, the energy, as you said, to overcome the intimidations, and I had written as you had suggested, "The story I would not want my mother and father to read," "The story I would not want Owen to read," "The story I would not want my daugh-

ters to read," and while I didn't use those titles, you proba
could tell which was which, and yes, in spite of some nega
ism in the technique (I was afraid of revealing myself,
I was not only afraid), writing with that impulse did get
past some of my inhibitions, although you seemed by th
assignments to be pushing me toward the "confession
poets even as in your suggestions for reading you steered
away from them, and you certainly (out of your theory
know, and I do believe that you believe in it, but I ne
quite understood it, after all it wasn't *my* theory, and y
had told me that style and meaning had reciprocal impli
tions, so that I could scarcely have your style imposed on
without having something of your meanings imposed on r
and even now if I think in terms of imposed versus imman
implications I could not tell where my thought began a
yours ended, and you would say that it didn't matter, tha
was just something you picked up from Whitehead or son
body, and you would refer me to your sources, but I thi
you were being elusive, not modest, and it was you I w
interested in, not Whitehead)—and now I have lost my id
and my syntax. Anyway your final suggestion to me,
write "The story I would not want Bill Wilson to read,"
took as your attempt to get rid of me, and I did not write
in fact I stopped writing, and I return to that theme no
only because I have wanted to write you a letter and ha
not had the self-stylization (I know you enjoy those German
phrases) or the point of view from which to write a lette
and you did stress point of view as the problem which woul
dissolve complacencies and resolve the story. So I needed a
excuse to write to you, and now looking over my stories an

your notes, tossing them into the fireplace and starting a fire with them in the evening—I have carried out the trash for the last time in my life—I see that you may not have meant me to stop sending stories, you may have meant me to reach beyond the awareness that you would be reading what I had been writing, to send it to you in spite of the implications of the title, you were trying to help me stop being afraid of you but also to transcend some painful self-limitation—and you did not want my fear of you to be your fault, but if it weren't, then it was only another painful weakness of my own—anyway I think that you were ambivalent about reading my things, I know you felt put upon by so many demands on your time—what you had been through with your marriage, and the children—and I was not used to courage, I was brought up not to ask for help, and I was lazy enough to find it easiest to read that title as an attempt to be rid of me. But now I have found the point of view, the excuse, for this letter, which will be my last story, and which is, in several senses but in no ambiguous sense, the story I would not want Bill Wilson to read—

—I knew when I saw you at that New Year's Eve reception —you looked aghast when you saw me sitting in the row of chairs arranged so formally along the wall, I suppose to make space and to make people behave themselves—that you had heard about the accident (I am tempted to delay here, but then I remember that each part of a story, each word if possible, was to work frontally as well as laterally, so I will not merely say *accident*, I will attempt something of that convex meniscus, to use one of the images you used for writing that you liked, which I know you said was just

[120]

CONVEYANCE

something you remembered from high-school chemistry, and didn't reflect any scientific experience or knowledge, but I never seemed to remember images like that from chemistry, still I got the point that surprise endings were out, that exposition was difficult if not impossible, that one had always to be *in medias res*), I knew that you knew that my husband and my daughters were dead, and how they had died, when I saw you standing there with a coat and tie among men in tuxedos and women in evening gowns, and I could retrieve from your denim shirt your calculations as to how close you could come to them without becoming too distant from yourself, and I saw the glass in your hand, and I don't know what you thought I was thinking, I had not responded to your last note or to your lengthy criticisms, my life had become a tragedy but I lacked a tragic sense of life, I was trying to look neither approachable nor unapproachable, I did not want to attend a New Year's Eve reception, of course, but in the easy paradoxes and formulas which make it so difficult to think about my experience, my absence would have been a presence, and I thought that I would make it easier on everyone by putting in a brief appearance early in the evening: and I wanted to be unfaithful to my grief. Looking at you—and I had not heard that you had been in the hospital, because friends stopped telling me sad or disquieting news, and I did not know that you had enough reasons for your own wintry desolations, and I don't know what we could have done for each other anyway, I don't know how we might have helped each other, I was as you might have noticed incapable of eating, and was already drinking, and looking at you I focused on the glass of ice in your hand,

[121]

probably plain soda water—if you have been waiting for
my charge of self-righteousness, here it is, I saw you standing
there in clothes which let you look the economic or social
inferior of people whom you undoubtedly felt superior to,
after you had lectured me against irony, and you drinking
nothing while others drank alcohol, or you drinking white
wine while they drank Scotch, I had been able to grasp your
self-righteousness on the level of these details—partly because
you tried to train me in concreteness, although my concrete
details often seemed to me illustrations of your generaliza-
tions about concrete details, and if I could catch, on the level
of concrete details, that you were much too much out to get
people, scanning for errors instead of applauding, I had more
trouble on more abstract levels because you were so practiced
at escaping, were if not glib at least well prepared, I think
you confused being correct with being good, so that I could
never make my point because you seemed determined to be
in the right whatever the cost, you were a Proteus who
changed shape if anyone tried to touch you, or if anyone did
touch you. I was saying that I was looking at the glass in your
hand and thinking of glass or of ice—I did not decide which
—as the failure of light, a line of imagery I knew you would
resist, although I did not know, as I have said, how sick you
had been, and perhaps you have changed. (I hear my assumption in that sentence, that suffering chastens. Sorry.) You
were trapped beside the mantlepiece by that man who produced ethnic records, I could see that struggle on your face
between boredom and searching for some fact to let him
know that you knew something about his subject—I say only
what you said first about yourself, that you knew most of

what you knew from book reviews, those self-accusations which forestalled accusations, deafening yourself to criticism, but it was true, you were often only as interesting as the most recent paperback you had read, though you did (do) have a flair for what you call your colloquial undercut, and I was (am) grateful for your explanations, I always thought that you were a good teacher, I never denied you that. I don't know which of us left the party first, I didn't see you when I said my thank-yous and good-nights.

I was not interested in a poem about a glass of ice and the frequencies of light, I knew in advance your comment, that if I had to work with such an image, to commit myself to its implications with precision, and I sat there remote from my own indictments of your self-protective and self-serving tact, your endless tact, I had grown, not compassionate, but beyond caring much about anything or anyone, I suppose one of "the indifferent children of the earth," to quote as you would quote so quickly a line from *Hamlet* that I would recognize but wouldn't have remembered aptly. I am writing now in a mood of indifferent festivity because death is ripening within my reach, just about my death of choice, cirrhosis, with the complication of hepatitis that I knew I could count on Mexico for, and an operation by the local "doctor" that I underwent as I would undergo an ultimate poem, and I will describe that later, but not to hurt you. I am trying not to terrorize you for your own good. I thought that I would be unable to write at all after the operation, for I haven't had the energy even to think, but somehow I have this surge which I suppose has some chemical base—I haven't even been able to drink for the last few days—so perhaps my body is consuming itself, I am saprozoic (at least I have *our* dictionary here with me, you might be amused to know)—and I guess my body is releasing its reserves of cortisone, or tapping its reservoir of adrenalin—although the truest image is from that W. C. Fields movie we all saw as part of that subscription series, where he burns up the wooden parts of the steamboat in its own steam engine in order to win the race—for beyond any adrenergics is the true source of energy, my nearness to my own death, I suppose you would say the energy of my position in relation to a force, although you would remind me here to think of the verb, *dying*, rather than the noun, *death*, you see I do remember, but also I do mean *death*, hitherto my most abstract relationship, but one that is becoming quite concrete. And no one can tell me what I am allowed to mean.

    I hope you will not think me cruel to write this description: the plane hopped such short distances, from island to island, that it should have been small and had two seats in each row, like a streetcar or a train, but it had three seats, so I sat at the window seat behind the row with Owen, Amy, and Elise in front of me, the girls taking turns at their window seat, although there was less and less to see as it grew darker, and I could almost see through the backs of their seats the excitement and pleasure, and I did see an occasional hand reaching between the seats, an occasional face peeking at me over the top of the seat, the girls so pale and thin, my daughters who would never be sturdy, the aloof or reserved look of sickly children underlying the normal eagerness of arriving in the night at a Caribbean island, and the plane landed on the water, a few passengers disembarked, and then it took off,

the last of the sunset, and then the last of the passengers
after we landed in the dark amidst small boats, and then the
anticipation as I remembered this flight with Owen ten
years before, and wondered about the wisdom of returning
to the island with the children, when we had known it only
without them, but I occupied myself thinking about the three
of them in front of me, and how I made four, or how Amy,
Elise, and I, three females, made three, the women Owen
wondered aloud how he could make happy, or as he used to
say sometimes, how he could shut us up, and Amy and
Elise were two together, daughters and sisters, sometimes as
different from me as boys, girls who were allowed to look
like boys sometimes, so unlike my childhood, my girlhood,
for which I still wanted reparations—I had had a layette and
a bassinet, and when I was at Goucher my mother was still
sending me lingerie from Altman's—although at least nothing in that girlhood tempted me to prolong it, so I am grateful for that—and Amy and Elise looked like each other, although Elise looked more like Owen, and Amy looked more
like me, especially after I had to get glasses for reading, so
that I could say that I was to Amy as Amy was to Elise as
Elise was to Owen, as though our children conveyed us to
each other, as their frail bodies bodied forth the sensitivities
we had both deliberately preserved in ourselves, although
not our physical strength, because they, in that ugly word I
hate so much, had that syndrome, although in my rage I
never could see the connection between their poor vision,
the brittle bones, and the allergies, I could not then understand what the doctors said because I knew they meant that
Amy and Elise would never be healthy, never eat a normal

meal, and that my complex love for my daughters would be complicated by pity and fear, while the attitude of our friends toward their sickness was too correct—some smell of liberal self-congratulation was in the air when they served the right foods without calling attention to their consideration—weren't they angry, like I was? Aren't they angry, like I am? I wanted to file a complaint somewhere. Several complaints.

The plane circled too long, even I could tell that, now that we were the last four passengers, thinking to myself once upon a time there was a woman and she had two daughters, they set out with her husband, their father, to find the island where . . . , and as the plane took too long I remembered that marvelous medical historian's story about flying over the Andes and looking round to see the stewardess stretched out on the floor in the aisle of the plane with a rosary held to her breast—he was doing research for a history of medicine in South America—and his stories seemed so riotously funny that evening in New Haven when he kept accidentally knocking the chairs and ashtrays out of alignment, until the whole hard-edged apartment was in subtle disarray, and I gave a surreptitious shove to the wooden triangle containing the antique billiard balls which Si had placed on the coffee table as an *objet trouvé* but consistent with his own aesthetic of sharp-focus geometry, I think you said that Si's Bauhaus managed to sublate Surrealism, as you used a word I had never heard anyone work into a conversation, I think you sublated a little Surrealism yourself, more than you knew, and I wanted to tell that evening how I used to shop in stores which had been a hundred feet or more below where we were then sitting, before the urban renewal had torn down that market street and put up that building with the first several storeys a parking garage, but I never got to describe myself as a good Fulbright wife shopping in the little markets instead of the supermarket for the ingredients of a peasant casserole I had learned to make that year abroad, I never got to tell my story or even later going down in the elevator past street level to the underground parking lot, and in some nervousness I admiringly took the lid off a primitive basket that Si with his incredible eye had bought in Brazil—something functional which had perfect classical lines and echoed his own prints or rhymed with the Barcelona chairs—but I didn't tell my story, I was feeling dowdy graduate-student wife, and remembering that your wife—you seemed less to have gotten married than to have joined the circus—had said that the wives of academic psychologists look like laboratory mice before she asked Owen what he studied, and he was embarrassed for her and for me, but they forgot her remark about mice because she was off on his midwesternism, and how men from the American midwest were the last men who knew how to walk like men without knowing that they were doing so—and in the hand-woven basket were Si's dirty clothes, he was furious that I had discovered that the object so perfectly deployed in an apartment which was more a still-life painting than a home was *functional*, and I thought only that he was clever to think of using it for a laundry basket and to keep it in the living room, and I sank back in my chair, I shrank, knowing that my posture was not making the chair look good—a plump-faced woman who looked as though if she were to lose twenty pounds she would be beautiful or at least pretty, but I have lost twice that much now. So it was one of those evenings, as though Si gave a party like that to prove his theory of people to himself all over again—and the plane was taking too long to land, we were off our schedule, and I was remembering nonsense, and why couldn't I have been like Charlotte when Warren upset her coffee table breaking all those cups and she said without a trace of irony, Oh that's all right, they were very old anyway, and I don't think Warren ever realized—and I came back from those memories to the row of seats in front of me, to the three, one of whom made me a wife, two of whom made me a mother, three of whom made me a woman in my own eyes, though I know that now that would be a counterrevolutionary thought and I wouldn't have wanted Amy and Elise to think like that when they grew up, and if I could make myself into a writer I don't know what that would make me, different from what I was yet more myself I hoped, but the ambition was important, and the plane was circling too long, the lone stewardess came back to say that the fog was thick and that we were running low on fuel and would land in the dark on calm seas, and of course we could depend upon ourselves to behave well, I had grown up with monograms on everything, I heard the clicks of the other three seat belts, the lights in the plane dimmed and went out, and we sat waiting in the vivid darkness.

When the plane touched I felt the smack of the impact and heard screams as the plane split along the seams, and lights came on in the forward section as it ripped free and sank while I was being lifted in my seat high into the air and

leaned over looking down onto Owen, Amy, and Elise reaching up, it was like looking down onto people on the seat below one on a ferris wheel as one held on for dear life, and
then the lights, the front half of the plane, and their faces
disappeared, and I sat tilted up in my end of the plane as it
gradually subsided, and I waited, silent and alone, trapped
in my lifeboat, until the sky bruised with light in the east,
and I can quote the Bible without worrying about all of the
implications: "And the heaven departed as a scroll when it
is rolled together; and every mountain and island were
moved out of their place." Nice, isn't it? And morning came
sooner than I could think, and my perplexed rescue by a
ship's boat, bobbing up and down in that truncated airplane,
not feeling lost, knowing that I was twenty-five thousand
miles to the east of myself, twenty-five thousand miles to the
west of myself, perhaps I could find myself if I decided to
look.

I flew, I was flown, back to New York. You had not heard
from me for a year, I saw no reason to get in touch. I drank
quietly and conscientiously, thinking of my liver turning as
orange as a life jacket. I will not repress these images, now
that I am capsizing, though I can hear you complaining
about women confessional poets dredging their hearts, and
I could quote you on how comparisons deplete the actuality of
the things compared. But I am now mistress of my own de-
pletions. I drank, but I underestimated my strength. God, I
was robust. I stayed in the city, selling the house, arranging
every detail, finally achieving an order so that everything
is as it will be after I have died, and here I have nothing that
I don't need for the next few days, the maid does everything,

[129]

and as I read through your letters and my poems and stories I toss them onto this comfortable fire. I could be out of this place in five minutes if I had to be.

I flew here, not because you had mentioned Río Caliente in a story, because after all you learned the name from me, though you left off the accent: Río. Everyone has been pleasant, I feel that I am almost a type they know how to handle me so well, they seem familiar with me (unless it is my familiarity with death that they sense; again I almost didn't say that—we discussed Lawrence, Bill, *The Plumed Serpent*, and you scored the points, but also you never heard me out). In any event (forgive my mischief—I know you hate the phrase) the state of medicine here is complicated—I could tell you of some acquaintances I drank with in the evening who had had incurable cancer in the States and here have been cured with Laetrile—they come back every year for triumphant vacations—and this isn't voodoo, but real doctors, trained in the States, who used medicines that weren't approved there, perhaps they are now, but anyway these people tell me about being examined—a *sigmoidoscopy*, no less—and about growths as big as grapefruits or oranges that have shrunk to the size of grapes—I love their gratitude as they talk about their operations, their Laetrile enemas, their "Wobe-Mugos" enzymes, and they told me how well I looked and discouraged me from drinking the water. I am so tired now I must get to the interesting part of my operation. I wanted nothing to do with the antiseptic young doctors at the one-story hospital they're all so proud of, but the maid told me about a local man who performs miraculous operations, and I agreed to see him for the entertainment. I underestimated him, however, for he is impressive, and if anyone wanted to be cured, he could probably do it, although he has enough sense to send some patients to the hospital, part of an understanding with the healthy young doctors that is beyond me. They just don't draw the line between appearance and reality at the same place you and I do, and perhaps both of us underestimated the amount of illusion in experience. I am not going to describe the operation I let him perform for my liver. He gave me marvelous stuff—I felt no pain, but if I wanted to be aware I could be, and if I didn't want to be, I could drift off, which I mostly did. A young boy stood by throughout, all expressionless intelligence, but when the medicine man was ready to sew me up, the boy stepped forward opening the box he held in front of his heart, and while my witch doctor apposed the edges of the incision, the boy would take out an enormous black ant, and when the ant had seized the edges with its mandibles, he would cut the thorax from the ant head, thus making one stitch. And so I was sutured with eighteen ants, a dozen miles from a hospital that is the pride of the Indians. And if truth were to be told, I have felt better—weak, but clear—since the operation, and I look at my incision with admiration, it seems to me an image of unquestionable beauty, an act of poetic truth, although I would not want to have to define my terms, and I don't have to.

I was going to go through your comments and answer some of them, quote them back to you: "the problem with the story is that you set up the situation so laboriously that

it is obviously a set-up. Try to get closer to magic than this:
something should appear without apparent cause, or be set
up before your eyes and you be disbelieving yet incapable
of disbelief. You will think that I merely lack a sense of
humor. . . ." But I don't want to estrange you. You will think
that *I* lack a sense of humor. I have two final points. First,
I have realized, while writing this letter and reading your
comments, that you had expected to learn from me, and
that part of your disappointment in me was not you as teacher
disappointed in me as student, but you as student disappointed in me as teacher, and I am willing to see now that
your saving grace has been that you always expected to
learn. Naïve of you, Bill, but I forgive you.

If what I have just written is true, and if you have not
known it, then you have learned something from me, and
perhaps I have not disappointed you entirely. And so my
second point if I am the teacher. You have been so articulate
that your attempts to lift me beyond intimidations were
themselves intimidating, though we discussed our fears about
writing, and I knew that I hurt you by being afraid of you.
Now I have told you my story, or enough of it, I feel more
good will than you might perhaps credit me with, and you
might say as you tirelessly said of my stories, at least of my
adjectives, that I should render the evidence, not render the
verdict, but anyway I am quite lively now, a woman who
successfully absconded to Mexico in order to abandon her
life, and I want you to do something for me that may do
something for you, and that is to accept from me the sort
of assignment that I used to accept from you. Now that you

have read my letter, write the story that you would want me to read. Goodbye, Bill. I'm going the rest of the way on my own.

Best regards,
C.

William S. Wilson was born in Baltimore, Maryland, and went to school in Baltimore and in Towson, Maryland. He was graduated from the University of Virginia, where he majored in the philosophy of science. He received a Ph.D. in English literature from Yale University. He has published numerous articles on painting and sculpture, and his stories have appeared in *Antaeus, New Directions, Paris Review,* and *TriQuarterly*. His story "Anthropology: What Is Lost in Rotation" was chosen for inclusion in *The Best American Short Stories 1977*. Mr. Wilson teaches in New York City, where he lives with his two daughters and one son.